Wasp Box

PANHANDLER
BOOKS
UNIVERSITY OF WEST FLORIDA | PANHANDLERMAGAZINE.COM

Wasp
Box

Jason Ockert

PANHANDLER
BOOKS
PENSACOLA, FLORIDA

This book may be available in an electronic edition.

20 19 18 17 16 15 6 5 4 3 2 1

Library of Congress Control Number: 2014913674
ISBN 978-0-9916404-0-9

Panhandler Books
Department of English and World Languages
Building 50
University of West Florida
11000 University Parkway
Pensacola, FL 32514
http://www.panhandlermagazine.com

University of
West Florida

For what's in your head

I.

The soldier pitches himself from the moving train. When he hits the ground his ankles turn, and he drops. He rolls down a slope and splays out beside the trunk of a tree. He breathes like he's trying to blow out a bonfire. Momentarily distracted by his disheveled body, the soldier fights to concentrate. Crosshaired by branches, the moon is passing through clouds. *It's the same old rock in the sky*, he tells himself. *Anyone anywhere can find it above.* This comforts a little. Enough to sit upright, fumble for his pack, and fetch his water. With blood-crusted fingers he lifts the canteen to his flaky lips. It's empty. And, just like that, the pain in his head returns.

"Shit," he says, finding his feet. He snatches a nearby twig and jams it into his right ear. Something is scuttling around inside his skull, and no matter how deeply he digs he just can't root it out.

While difficult, on those ankles, the soldier runs. Since he cannot fight, he flees. He should watch where he steps. He should move with stealth. He should reach for his firearm and be concerned when he finds it is gone and then he should remember that he is home or nearly home. This is the United States of America. It's time to segue back to citizen. Leave overseas overseas. It's unwise to carry ghosts across the ocean.

Things from his pack drop to the forest floor as he forges ahead. Branches snag his clothing and whip his face and neck. He tears through spider webs and thinks, *The itsy-bitsy spider crawled up the waterspout*— he used to sing this to his sister, Kylie. She was the one that helped him stave off loneliness; maybe she can help him battle back the pain. *Down came the rain . . .*

If he were in a better state of mind the soldier would notice signs of the small river before stumbling upon it: the telltale rivulet murmur, the damp smell in the air, the small patches of moss glistening in the moonlight. Instead, he is nearly knee-deep in the water before he realizes it. Gratefully, he dunks his head beneath the surface. The burning in his lungs feels tremendous, and he does not want to rise—*wash the spider out*. If only he could stay submerged forever dousing the writhing embers in his skull. Underwater provides a moment of clarity. *Rivers lead to people*, he reasons. *Surely there's a medic just around the bend. There's nothing wrong with me a jab of morphine wouldn't fix—out came the sun to dry up all the rain . . .* Unable to fight any longer, the soldier breaks from the surface, choking. Somehow he has gotten water in his mouth. Sloshing to shore, he alternates between hard swallowing and raw heaving. Like a drunk, he staggers to a tree that keeps him propped up as he gets sick. Even when he thinks he's emptied out and done, he's not. He gags, slumps to his knees—*Oh, God, please*—and tries to offer more. To the soldier's great surprise, he hacks out bits of something into his cupped hands. Through watery eyes, he tries to make out what he's got: it looks like a half-dozen prunes. *Maybe this is what's been causing the pain. Maybe I ate something awful. Maybe this old body just needed to cleanse itself, get rid of the poison I took in while away. Now that I'm back . . .* the soldier's line-of-reasoning is called into question when his focus narrows and the objects in his hands move. Then, tiny red-tinted wings unfurl and the creatures unsteadily take flight. For a baffling moment, the soldier thinks this is all rather beautiful. He has made something here.

The moment does not last long. The soldier will learn the difference between being the creator of life and the incubator of it. He has trouble breathing again, his nasal passages clog, and the urge to simultaneously swallow and cough returns. With all of his strength he resists . . . *and the itsy-bitsy spider climbs up the spout again.* He squeezes his lips tight even as his mouth fills with the curious insects stinging and fighting to get out.

. . . climbs up the spout again . . .

With his eyes pinched shut the soldier cannot see what's been eating him up inside push past his pliable lips and perch momentarily there before taking flight. The wasps are like wicked words—the soldier's confession—made manifest. They rise away and whisper to the moon.

2.

Hudson's father is waiting at the station. Through the train window the young man can see his dad standing apart from the thin crowd, hunching over his lighter to ignite his cigarette. Even at this distance the boy can place the scent of the Marlboro on his father's breath, and this memory sends a quick wave of anxious heat from his chest to his head. It's been two years since he saw his dad who traveled to New York City for a long weekend. During that last visit Hudson was so grateful to see his old man that he sat with his back straight in the diner booth and spoke to his father like he was being interviewed. When smoke from his father's cigarettes drifted into his face, Hudson didn't blink or choke or blow it away. Now, swiping at the droplets of sweat beading on his forehead, Hudson nudges his half-brother sleeping beside him.

The boy stirs but doesn't wake. He's wearing headphones and has classical music playing softly. The music helps lull him to sleep. Hudson can see faint ripples on Speck's eyelids beneath which his eyes are darting, caught up in a vivid dream. Lately, since witnessing a bicyclist get hit by a cab, Hudson's younger brother has been battling night terrors. Most nights, Hudson can crawl out of the lower bunk bed, climb the ladder, and nestle himself next to his little brother in the top bed. The boy will gnash his teeth and curl his hands into rigid claws and moan guttural while thrashing his legs. Hudson does his best to hold onto the boy and just ride it out. In the morning, Speck won't remember a thing. And though it might be a mistake, Hudson hasn't said a word to their mother.

There is some debate about which boy looks more like their mother.

Hudson has her cheekbones and nose, and Speck has her eyes and long, curly, red-tinted hair. Speck's given name, Joshua, named after his father's father, nobody but teachers use. Apparently, as the story goes, when his stepfather brought Hudson to the hospital to see his little brother swaddled in his mother's arms, Hudson, seven at the time, had said, "He's just a speck of a thing," and this comment sent his mother into a bout of laughter that ended up rousing the infant and sending him into a howling rage. The boy still doesn't much care for the nickname.

"Hey," Hudson says, plucking a headphone from Speck's ear, "we're here."

Before they left this morning Hudson's mother had taken him aside and asked, "Do you know why I'm *really* letting you go see him now?"

Hudson knew better than to answer. The fact that his mother agreed to allow them both to go is a small miracle. It was Hudson's stepfather who ended up convincing her. Hudson could earn summer money, and Speck could use the fresh country air, he reasoned. To sweeten the pot, the stepfather bought tickets for a cruise to the Bahamas. It's a trip they've been meaning to take for years. The plan is to drive over in early August, pick up the boys, and then tour several colleges and universities in the area for Hudson to consider. Instead of answering his mom this morning, Hudson shrugged.

"Because you're old enough to discover for yourself what a lousy man your father is," she said.

As the passengers file off the train Hudson pinches Speck's elbow. "Wake up," he says, loudly.

Startled, the boy's eyes pop open. He sucks in a little drool that has accumulated in his mouth. His sweat-drenched hair has been flattened by the hard, worn, plastic seat. He fumbles with his headphones.

"What were you dreaming about?"

"I don't know," the boy answers. "Are we here?"

"If you don't tell me what you were dreaming right this instant you'll forget forever."

"It's not important. I don't even remember, Hud."

"I was watching you. Something was going on up there." Hudson gently taps Speck's forehead.

"Leave me alone," the boy says, sliding into the aisle. "Is that your dad?"

Hudson turns his attention back to the window where his father is grinding out the cigarette on the platform. Hudson is surprised how little his old man has changed. His deep-set dark eyes are scanning the windows, his brown hair still has gray streaks, and he's wearing the same old jeans and simple green T-shirt he might have worn last time. He is a perfect reproduction of how Hudson remembers him. Right now he's leaning forward as if anticipating a shove from some stranger.

Before his father's eyes can alight on him, Hudson stands and hurries his brother along. "Let's go."

Outside, it is dusk, and the air is trying to recover from the scorch of the day. The state of New York has been mired in a heat wave, and the past week has been particularly brutal to the Finger Lakes region.

Having discarded his cigarette, Hudson's father can't decide what to do with his hands. First, he clasps them together behind his back, and then he places them on his hips before deciding to cram them into his pockets. What he'd like to do is get the introductions over with and head home for a drink to calm the nerves.

Thirteen years ago Nolan told his wife he couldn't do it anymore.

"Do what?" Erin asked, tiredly.

"This," he said, meaning the commission-based pharmaceutical sales job, the cramped studio apartment, the heavy-footed upstairs neighbors, the two kittens she'd rescued from the trash compactor, the way his son was always underfoot. "And my migraines have returned."

Erin, who had heard all of this before, said, "It's called a hangover."

In response Nolan raised his hand to strike her, an instinct that surprised him more than it did her.

Ashamed, he packed a suitcase and left. Later, when he talked with Hudson on the phone, he'd say he always intended on returning. Maybe things would have been different if Erin wasn't so quick to remarry. She'd found a replacement husband before the ink on the divorce papers had time to dry.

Hefting their packs, the boys climb off the train. Hudson follows Speck slowly down the stairs in order to seem less eager. He wants time to take in his father's face as they arrive.

Speck humps over to Nolan and extends his hand. "It's good to see you again, Mr. Baxter."

Nolan takes the boy's hand and crushes it. "Likewise, Mr. Petro."

"Hey, Dad," Hudson says.

"That hurt," Speck says, shaking his hand away.

"Come here," Nolan says, embracing his son. Nolan can only reach halfway around because of Hudson's backpack. "I've missed you."

"Me, too," Hudson replies.

Pulling away, Nolan says, "Let me look at you. Nearly a man now, huh? Scrawny as I used to be. Who taught you how to shave—a cat claw your face?"

Hudson's smiling lips quiver. "I'm still learning."

"Always use a sharp blade. Don't skimp on shaving cream. I'll show you. You too, Mr. Petro. Peach fuzz."

"Sure," the boy says still massaging his hand. "Do you mind just calling me Speck?"

"Any more bags?" Nolan asks.

"Nope."

"Good. I'm over here." Nolan's ratty-brown pickup truck is parked toward the rear of the parking lot. As they approach, Speck asks, "Can I ride in the back?"

"That's fine. Mind the sign, though."

Speck hurries to the bumper and throws himself up into the bed. He has to sit squished next to an enormous sign that reads, WIDE LOAD, a necessity for Nolan's job following big rigs that carry prefabricated trailer homes up and down the I-90 and I-81 corridors. Speck smiles and says, "I've got a teacher you could carry this behind."

"Good one," Hudson says, reaching out to ruffle his brother's hair.

"You want to drive?" Nolan dangles the keys.

"Sure," Hudson doesn't hesitate although he does not have his license. His stepfather has taken him to empty parking lots a few times; he's got the hang of it.

Nolan discovered Dwyer by accident. After leaving New York City he traveled to Ohio and moved in with his parents. He didn't expect to stay long, but his father became ill, and he found himself trying to salvage the lukewarm relationship he'd always had with the old man by sticking around, watching ball games, arguing about the proper way to maintain their small, weedy front lawn. His father's passing motivated Nolan to work on his own relationship with his son. Climbing into his car he convinced himself he was going to return to New York City, get back into sales, and rent a little place where he could entertain Hudson on weekends. On the way back, Nolan's head began to pound. He was forced to pull over and check into a hotel where he stayed for a week. Every evening he'd sit in a rocking chair on a balcony overlooking the water, cigarette in hand, and talk himself into finishing the drive in the morning.

The Muller vineyard is set back a half-mile off of County road 89. A sign with the Muller Wineries insignia—a burgundy M atop a black W, like a series of peaks and valleys with a diamond in the center—stands weather-beaten along the side of the road.

"This is us," Nolan says to Hudson.

Just off 89 is the first house on the property. The structure stands towering in the dwindling light and throws shadows like a bruise over a small parking area out front. This is where the majority of the business is run. In the front, with unimpeded views of Seneca Lake, is an extensive porch with rocking chairs and tables and a swing. Most wine tasters sit outside when the heat isn't unbearable. Inside the front, public portion of the house is a small gift shop where you can buy a number of knick-knacks promoting the region—coffee mugs, magnets, T-shirts, decorative spoons—and several varieties of Muller wine. There is also a raised bar that runs the length of the room facing the window and the water. This serves as a place for patrons to taste wine and order a sandwich or salad, just a small meal that Ms. Muller will make when she is in the mood. Behind the shop are the private quarters where Clara and her daughter Madison live. The heart of the business is attached to the house and spirals down to the cellar and the distillery. All the aging, bottling, labeling, and boxing are done in the cool of the underground. The cellar backs up to a loading dock that also holds a small office. It's too early in the season to hire workers for the harvest and, for now, the business can be managed with just a handful of employees.

The vineyard occupies seventy acres of land extending from 89 east through a small forest and the railroad, north to an apple orchard, and south to county road 96. The ground pitches slightly down a slope and feeds into the trees. Neatly organized rows of grapes stack up side-by-side and stretch the horizon. Each row is made up of fifty, five-foot posts spaced six feet apart. The posts are connected by three taut wires: one near the top, one in the middle, and one at the bottom. Vines intertwine with the wires to form a patchy verdant tapestry. This early in the season the fruit is young and green and growing strong with dime-sized orbs. At the end of each row are blooming rose bushes; vintners use the sweet fragrance of the flowers to divert insects away from their crop.

Nolan instructs Hudson down a dirt road set back from the main house. The pockmarked path grades down a small hill and forks. To one side, it angles toward a large barn. To the other side, it leads to a second, smaller house. The paint on the structure used to be red and is now chipped and faded nearly pink. Whereas the front home stands tall against the horizon, the pink house is shrinking under the expanse of fields.

After years of military service in World War II, Gustave Muller and his wife Elizabeth returned to the States. At the time, there were only a handful of wineries in the Finger Lakes and the Muller's used the modest funds they'd accumulated to buy land and try to cultivate the earth. Gustave's great grandfather owned a vineyard in the Burgundy region of central France that had managed to survive the war. Though the process took years and years of cross-hybridization between the Burgundy vine and the regions better-established Catawba and Isabella species, the Muller's were able to produce a distinctive product—the *Muller Roux*— with which to build a modest reputation.

"You live in a pink house?" Speck shouts through the back window as he jostles in the bed of the pickup.

"It's red," Nolan says. "Just faded."

There is a dilapidated wrap-around porch with two rocking chairs in the front of the house facing the vineyard. The beaten road cuts from the house to the barn and then bisects the rows of grapes on its way to the forest. The tallest trees sway in the still-warm breeze. By now, it is evening, and the landscape is bathed in the last light of the day. Hudson parks. "It's nice," he says, meaning it.

Having heard them coming, two German Shepherds—one black, one white—burst from behind the barn and tear up the road.

"Um," Speck says, staying in the bed. "Mr. Baxter, are those friendly?"

"Depends, Mr. Petro," Nolan says, "how hungry they are."

The dogs arrive behind a chorus of quick barks. Hudson extends his hands palm up for the animals to sniff. They settle down enough for

Nolan and Hudson to pat their heads. Speck stays suspicious in the safety of the pickup.

"Black one is Sultan, white one is Pepper. You'll get used to them."

"Are they yours?"

"Gus looks after them, but they pretty much take care of themselves. They make good companions. Keep them out of the house, though."

"Guys?" Speck calls. "Don't leave me here." Satisfied that Hudson isn't a threat, the dogs are clawing at the pickup and trying to get to the boy.

"They're fine. Put your palms out. Let them sniff you."

"I don't want to," Speck says, his voice breaking.

Hudson hears the panic and returns to help his brother out. He sets his bags down so he can scoop his brother up and carry him inside the house.

"They probably just smell the cats on you," Nolan says.

"What cats?" Speck asks.

"Don't you still have cats? Erin loved them."

"Steve's allergic," Hudson says.

"Ah," Nolan says. "I see. Well, you'll get used to them, Mr. Petro. Let me show you inside."

Downstairs is Nolan's apartment. From the foyer, to the left, there is a living area with a beige couch and a loveseat situated in front of a fireplace. The mantle is an old railroad tie fastened to the wall, and three wooden boxes sit upon it. Beyond the living room is a den lined with bookshelves, a leather couch, and a rocking chair. To the right of the foyer is a modest kitchen with a small table and an extended countertop under which two stools stand. Down a short hall off the living room are two bedrooms and a bathroom. The entire place is floored with scuffed hardwood, and there are rugs in every room except for the kitchen. On the walls are pictures of the vineyard in different seasons, at different times, all set in simple black frames.

"Your room is down there," Nolan says, pointing. "It's nothing fancy. Go get settled, and I'll make us something to eat."

In the room are two twin beds, with a nightstand between them, and a desk with a foldout chair beneath a window overlooking the fields.

"Not a lot of personality," Speck says as he throws his things on the bed closest to the window. "I don't even see a television."

"I get that bed," Hudson says. "Maybe there's a television in the living room."

"Did you see one?"

"No. But I wasn't looking. It won't kill us to go without. Besides, you've got your laptop. You can plug into your game. By the way, Mom told me you can only spend two hours a day playing. I don't plan on keeping track."

"What if I want to go home?"

"You better decide right now. Cruise leaves tomorrow. If you're going to chicken out, I need to know so I can get you back on the train. It's your choice. But once you've decided, you're committed. You may actually have fun. Did you see that lake? It's beautiful. Then there's the field and the forest, plenty of things to explore."

"What about the dogs?"

"Harmless once they get to know you."

"I just didn't picture it like this."

"Well," Hudson says, "now you know." He hands Speck his cell phone. "We promised we'd call when we arrived. You do it. I'm going to help my dad. Let me know your decision once you've made it."

Nolan is in the kitchen uncorking a bottle. He smiles when he sees Hudson. "I can't get over how much you look like I used to look."

Hudson takes a seat on a stool at the counter. "Got any old pictures?"

"Not here. Your mom might still have one or two. Unless she burned them all," Nolan says, smirking. "She ever let you drink wine?"

"Mom's not here."

"I'm glad you are, son."

"Me, too."

"Pot pies are in the oven."

"Great. I'm starving. You ever entertain anyone here?"

Nolan sets two milk glasses on the counter. "What's that supposed to mean?"

"Just curious. Could get kind of lonely."

"I manage."

"What about Gustave?"

"It's Gus. He won't set a foot in here."

"Why?"

"Never you mind. Sometimes you need to give a man his privacy."

Nolan fills his glass to the brim and pours a swallow for his son. He slides Hudson's cup across the counter. "Just a taste. Don't drink to get drunk."

"Yeah, right," Hudson says.

"What's that supposed to mean?"

"Nothing. So what's the plan tomorrow?"

"You think you can just change the subject and placate me?" Nolan raises an eyebrow and takes a gulp.

Hudson feels a constellation of sweat speckling his forehead. The pot pies are beginning to burn. "No, no. You just barely poured me anything. It's no big deal." In an effort to move on he raises his glass. "Here's to the summer."

Nolan lifts his own glass and stares hard into his son's eyes; they are nearly the same color. He can see his boy fighting the urge to look away. "Something you should know," the man says slowly. "Whenever you make a toast, maintain eye contact."

"All right," Hudson says, blinking. The two touch glasses. "Cheers."

"And don't be in such a hurry," Nolan takes a drink and turns his attention to the oven.

Hudson lets the wine linger, feeling the burn. He has had better. For now, though, it forces him to keep his mouth shut and let his father have the final word.

3.

The Finger Lakes Winefest is always well attended when it falls on the Fourth of July. Children sprint along the water's edge and fall without a care into the cold lake. Under a pavilion the band plays ragtime louder than it should be played. Hidden in a copse of trees teenagers light ladyfingers and bottle rockets. The parking lot has been transformed into an outdoor food court where local restaurants vie for business. The annual Best Burgers and Hots contest is under way. The winner receives a brass-polished trophy in the shape of a hamburger bun (something to display in the victor's restaurant window throughout the year). The air sizzles.

All up and down the pier, which juts out into Seneca Lake, are the wine tents. This year there are over twenty local vineyards represented. They've driven the short distance here from the other wineries dotting several of the Finger Lakes—Cayuga, Canandaigua, Keuka, Conesus, and Hemlock.

At the very end of the pier, Madison Muller is filling small, transparent, plastic cups with a sweet-tasting blush she knows will attract visitors in the suffocating heat. This far out there's a cool breeze lifting off the water. People can stand against the railing and admire the view. It's Madison's job to make sure they're holding a cup of one of the Muller Wineries most popular blends, *Icicle Rouge*—an ice wine that always draws a summer crowd.

Madison's curly-brown hair blows across her eyes. She tries to shake it away while arranging the free samples at the front of the table, and this causes the many bracelets on her arm to rattle. She is not yet used to the sound. The bracelets are covering a bandage on her wrist.

A recent graduate of Dwyer High, Madison is in a hurry to put distance between school life and her working life. Having grown up here Madison knows everyone, and everyone knows her, and it's all so stifling. If it weren't for the family business she'd be gone in a heartbeat. Ever since her grandmother passed Madison's mother has relied more and more on her to help run the business. The family name on the bottle is not without tarnish. Many years ago Clara partied with the drummer from a bluegrass band, ended up getting pregnant, and dropped out of school. Gus and Elizabeth circled the wagons and helped Clara raise Madison, but the town expressed their dismay every chance they got by slurring the Muller name in an attempt to drive business away. By the time she reached third grade kids were already branding Madison a bastard, having learned the word from their parents. Then, five years ago, her grandmother committed suicide. The reason she took her own life—doctors discovered a tumor in her brain that Elizabeth had no interest in combating—didn't matter to her peers. The older kids get the sharper their tongues become.

Now, though, having turned eighteen last week, Madison is officially an adult. She's mature enough to ignore the whispers and concentrate on the business, to be proud of the name on the label upon the bottle.

Two women with deep tans take quick shots of *Icicle Rouge*. Madison forces a smile. "We're offering a special today, if you're interested. Buy one get one half off."

"Let's think about it," one woman says, reaching for another sample. "May I?"

Madison doesn't bother answering. While she was never much of a student, she considers herself talented at reading people. Working at the gift store has given her much practice. She can tell by the way a woman purses her lips and averts her eyes that she is only interested in a bargain. The way a man gargles before swallowing during a taste test, looking furtively to see if anyone is watching and wondering if he is doing it right; this reveals a whole history Madison has come to interpret. He is a simpleton, a beta, the kind of man who has scurried into the arms of an overbearing woman. That overbearing woman, sitting beside him, will notice that he has no idea how to properly taste the wine, and she will quickly correct him. She wants more of the tasty crackers and will, if Madison can work the angle right, buy a novelty item with a grinning grape on it.

The problem with reading people is that everyone eventually becomes predictably dull. Like these two women who are reaching for their third cup and who are still pretending to be considering whether or not to buy a bottle. Madison tucks her hair behind an ear and takes in the atmosphere. Boaters anchored in the shallows toss their children overboard. Several kites made to resemble the flag dip and bob in the air currents. A group of light-skinned tourists pass by Madison, and she can smell the coconut scent from their sunscreen. Other tents are decorated with balloons and robust signs. The Muller tent simply has the insignia embossed on the overhanging tarp. Clara insists that if they are going to do this stupid festival every year they are going to do it with a modicum of integrity. Despite her mother's pessimism Madison is in a good mood. She has plans for the night. Her friend Beverly, a college student who works part time at the vineyard, has invited her to a party down in Ithaca. It is far enough away to possibly be fun.

Madison spots her mother making her way down the pier with Nolan. Clara is wearing a checkered blue sundress and a broad, straw hat. She has her good pearl necklace on and matching earrings. The mother is striking—she turns heads—and stays fit by never sitting still. Clara smiles, a phony smile Madison knows, and spits quick fragments of chitchat to the vintners manning the tents. She cannot stand a single one of them.

Sometimes it is difficult for Madison to read Clara. It is not always as easy as it is now in a crowd of people. A shrewd businesswoman, Clara adjusts her mood to those around her. Her public persona makes understanding her private personality—those moments when her blank expression and cold, half-lidded eyes slip into long, hollow stares—impossible for Madison to translate. Having Nolan around has helped tremendously.

The women loitering at the Muller tent mention that they may be back later and then stumble along the uneven wooden slats of the pier toward land. Clara and Nolan approach, and Madison realizes that the young man and boy walking a few paces behind are with them. The young man hides his hands in jean pockets, and his wide sunglasses reflect the world back to anyone who looks at him. The boy is pale. He's wearing shorts that are too big which he keeps tugging up. He's got on headphones, and his face is tightly concentrated on the music.

"Would you like to try a bottle of our *Icicle Rouge*?" Madison asks playfully. She holds a bottle outstretched like a trophy.

"I've had it before," Clara says. "It tastes like shit. Oh," she interrupts herself, "I probably shouldn't swear."

"You're fine," Nolan says. "He's not listening," Nolan nods his head to the boy.

"Yes I am," Speck says, removing the headphones. "I'm from the city. I've heard *shit* before."

"All right," Clara says. "I like your spunk, little man."

"I'd like you to meet Hudson and Mr. Petro," Nolan says to Madison. "They're going to be staying with me for the summer."

"Mom mentioned it," Madison says. She sets the bottle down, wipes her hands on a towel next to a cooler, and extends a hand. Speck is quick to take it. He wants to practice squeezing hard to, in a way that doesn't entirely make sense, get back at Hudson's dad.

"Oh, you've got quite a grip, Mr. Petro," Madison says, applying more pressure. When the boy tries to pull away she refuses to release. Eventually, as they both twist and squirm, they separate, laughing.

Hudson removes his hand from pocket long enough to raise it as a show of greeting. "Just call him Speck."

"The visit isn't just a vacation," Nolan says. "Hudson's got a job in construction which starts tomorrow, and I was hoping maybe you could find something for the boy."

"Sure," Madison says, "he can always clean the toilets."

"No way," Speck protests.

"And," Clara says, "I was wondering if you wouldn't mind taking Hudson with you to the party tonight?"

"Don't feel obligated," Hudson says, cutting in.

"Yeah, of course. No problem. I can't guarantee that it will be fun."

"If it's not an inconvenience."

"Not at all," Madison says. She tucks her loose hair back, and the clink of the bracelets reminds her to be careful how she moves.

"Hudson is considering colleges in the area, and I thought it might be helpful if . . ." Nolan says.

"I'm happy to have the company, really."

"Can I come?" Speck asks.

"Thanks," Hudson says.

"I'll wander over at eight."

"Can I come?"

"I don't know about you boys," Nolan says, "but I'm festivaled out. Clara, I'll see you back at the house later tonight?"

"What am I going to do?" Speck asks.

"Yes, you will," Clara says.

"Oh, there's plenty to do on the vineyard and in the woods," Madison says. "From our front porch you have the best view of the fireworks without having to fight the crowds. Plus," Madison motions for Speck to come close so she can whisper, "my grandfather always has something up his sleeves for a grand finale. You wait and see."

"What about the dogs?"

"They like fireworks, too."

"Come on. That's not what I meant. Are they friendly?"

"Yes," Madison says, seriously. "Give them a chance, and you'll see that they make better companions than humans."

"Thanks," Hudson says, again.

4.

After lunch at the festival the guys return home. What wind there was in the morning is gone now. The dogs loll under the shade of the barn. Inside the barn, a loud utility fan blows the air around. The old man stoops over a canvas propped upon a new easel. His derby-handled mahogany cane leans on a nearby stool. Before being rescued, Gus spent eight days in a German torture box in which he could not stand fully erect nor could he recline into a sitting position, and this has irrevocably damaged his knees. He tries very hard to remember that, if he didn't get captured and subsequently saved, he never would have met Elizabeth. Now that she's gone, every step he takes threatens to transport him back to those sealed up memories in the box half-standing and half-sitting, half-alive and half-dead.

Not long after his wife took her own life right here, in the barn that used to house farming equipment, Gus converted the structure into a hangar. There is enough room at the main house for anything they need for the business. With considerable help from veteran friends who knew people who knew people, and in the aftermath of his loss, Gus managed to track down, purchase, and have delivered (without the armament) a B-26 Martin Marauder—the *Widowmaker*. The irony of the gesture was not lost on Gus.

There was nothing particularly special about being a bombardier in WWII who got shot down and captured, which Gus was, but his wife Elizabeth became a war hero for her contributions in the Air Force. As a member of the Women Air Force Service Pilots (WASPs), Elizabeth was one of only about one thousand women who actively served. Her name is listed in history books. She piloted Gus out of Germany for good and, together, they never looked back. As per the neatly scripted and hand-written instructions on her suicide note, Gus saved half of her ashes in an urn (which he keeps on a bedside table and which will be combined with half of his own ashes and scattered in the fields when the time comes), and had the rest shipped to Arlington National Cemetery (where she awaits the other half of his remains).

For many hours during many months Gus would sit in the cockpit or else underneath in the bombardier's compartment or off the wing and daydream. He wasn't prepared for what the plane dredged up. More of-ten than not, instead of recollecting the particulars of Elizabeth at the controls and fearless, Gus slipped into the horrors of his own missions. As an airman, from above, he had the luxury of distance from the en-emy. Through the years, however, that distance began to collapse. His imagination filled in the blank faces of the deceased with acquaintances and friends he knew long ago. Spooked, he closed the hangar door and retreated back to the house. Staying in the house, without Elizabeth, was its own brand of torture. One morning the water in the tub wasn't draining properly, and when Gus bent down with a bent hanger to poke around and unclog it he fished out a soggy and putrid clump of his wife's hair. He'd gotten sick. Then, refusing his daughter's invitation to move into the main house (there's plenty of room), Gus moved up into the old apartment they used to rent out to seasonal grape harvesters. With his bad knees, it takes Gus five minutes to climb the stairs, but it's bet-ter than living haunted and alone below. Plus, Nolan arrived to rent the downstairs. Having him around provided a welcomed diversion. They'd spend evenings on the porch getting drunk. Gus tried to get involved with the business, which had changed, he knew, and he was more of an impediment than anything else. The new wine was not what he had imagined it might be; it had not aged as he hoped. The world was slid-ing by. *If Beth were still here*, he told himself, *she'd say, "Get a hobby."*

One cold day in February, Gus forced the hangar doors open against the drifting snow and stepped inside. Instead of climbing into the plane, he decided to paint it. Rather, he would paint portraits of the plane how he remembered it in the early 1940s using the way that the plane looked to him now as a bridge into the past. He started small and took his time and tried to capture each part of the B-26 with silver and red and black and yellow oils on canvas. Hanging on the barn walls are gallery-wrapped paintings of the Pratt & Whitney engines, the four-blade propellers, fixed machine guns on both port and starboard, a top turret, and several renderings of the bombardier's compartment. He paints with Elizabeth looking on. Now, as Nolan, Hudson, and Speck step into the hangar to say hello, Gus is scratching out the particulars of the landing gear.

Nolan says something the old man can't hear over the roar of the fan.

"Keeps my hands busy," Gus says loudly. "You know what they say about idle hands."

"I do," Nolan replies. "Looks good."

"I'm no Van Gogh." Gus wipes his hands on his paint-splattered pants and sets the brush aside. "These your boys?"

"Sort of," Nolan shouts. "Big one's mine. Hudson. Little one isn't."

"Thanks for letting us stay here," Hudson yells.

"Does it fly?" Speck asks, staring at the plane.

"Not anymore."

"Can I get in?"

Gus looks at his feet. Wind is whipping what's left of his gray hair. A brown droplet of paint drips down onto the hard-dirt barn floor. "Maybe later," he says. His voice is nearly lost in the noise.

"You'll be up at the house tonight?" Nolan asks.

"Wouldn't miss it."

"You've got a great piece of land," Hudson says.

"It's all right. Something to return to."

"What lives in those woods?" Speck asks, pointing.

"Son, there's only one way to answer a question like that."

"Can we go?" Speck asks Nolan.

"Your brother's your keeper."

Hudson gazes through the parted doors and down the dirt road bending into the trees. "I don't see why not."

"Have fun," Gus says. "Take the dogs."

As if on cue Sultan and Pepper appear in a wedge of shade beside the barn. When the boys set off, the dogs follow. Lining the road are the rows of grapes. Thick vines coil and sprout just barely contained by the wire. A tall, electric fence hems in the back of the vineyard. There is a *Danger* sign posted.

"What do you think that's for?" Speck asks.

"Deer, probably." Hudson's sneakers scuff the packed earth as he tries to figure out how to walk properly.

"Couldn't they just go around?"

Hudson ignores his brother as they enter the forest. A short distance beyond the tree line the road ends at a vehicle graveyard. Old rusted trucks and tractors are slowly decomposing. Most of the windshields have been busted and glass glints in the thickets of dying grass. Speck scampers ahead of Hudson, the dogs giving chase, to a Studebaker. The driver's side door is ajar, and it groans when he pulls it wider so he can slide onto the ripped upholstery and clutch the wheel. He hammers at the horn that relinquishes a limp bleat and nothing more. He roots around the backseat and discovers a few paper clips and bottle caps. In the ashtray he discovers a pocketknife. He has to work hard to pry the blade open. He wiggles it up and down until some of the rust falls away and then, closed, he hides it in his sock and steps out into a patch of weeds.

Hudson climbs into a faded yellow harvesting truck and sits behind the wheel. He lets the smell of oil, gasoline, baked-in sweat, and the faint waft of cigarette smoke seep in. The cushion has been slashed and stuffing spills around the pedals. Plastic on the dashboard is peeling off. The glove box handle is hot to the touch. Hudson uses the tips of his fingers to open it. Inside are a half-dozen charred Barbie dolls that have melted into one grotesque body. All of the hair has been singed, and the faces are smooth and expressionless. There's an old pink lighter deeper in the compartment amidst a nest of cigarette butts. Trying to puzzle through the logic of the remains, Hudson is distracted by his brother.

"Hey, Hud, what do they say about idle hands?" Speck is kicking around a pile of rocks.

Hudson slams the glove box closed and lets what's inside stay a mystery. "They're the devil's tools."

"What does that mean?"

"If you don't find something productive to do with your time you may become lazy." Hudson exits the truck and wipes sweat from his brow. "I see a trail up ahead. Let's take it and get out of the sun."

"I'll catch up," the boy responds. He watches his brother high-step a bundle of sticks and disappear into the forest. There is a rock pile near an old outhouse and from it Speck pulls stones the size of his fist and wings them at the tanker. The dogs sniff around, bored by the boy's bad aim.

Most of the rocks bounce off the hood without leaving a dent. Eventually, Speck connects with the windshield where a small crater forms in the glass. "That stinks," he says. "We were hoping for a little more boom, huh, boys?"

When Speck glances over at the dogs he sees Pepper pawing at the rotted baseboard of the outhouse. From his vantage, Speck can peer inside the structure and there, affixed to the buckled wood of the ceiling, hangs a watermelon-sized beehive. Pausing only for a second, rock poised in his hand, he shouts "Run!" and heaves the thing. It is a good throw. Bees explode from the outhouse quicker than Speck imagined. He stumbles as he backs away—swatting at the buzzing in his ears—sprints around a junked tractor and leaps over the thicket, laughing like a lunatic as he hurries to catch up to his brother on the trail. The dogs nip at his heels and bark excitedly.

In no time, the path becomes difficult for Speck to follow, and he is forced to slow down. The dogs stay in single file behind him. Just when it seems that the trail is going to be swallowed by the underbrush, the forest breaks to a slight rise that leads to a railroad track. Hudson is standing between ties and craning his head to listen to something. When Speck calls out, Hudson quiets him.

"Voices," Hudson says.

Speck scampers next to his brother and tries to hear what Hudson hears.

"Let's keep going," Hudson says.

A sudden loud explosion issues from the forest ahead and surprises both of the boys. The dogs perk their ears.

"Was that a gun?" Speck asks in a whisper.

"Fireworks."

"Oh yeah," the boy says. "I forgot it was the 4th. Mom and dad are out at sea by now."

"You made the right decision to stay."

"Did our train come in on these tracks?"

"I don't know," Hudson says. "Probably."

"Which way is Penn station?"

Hudson squints at the sky. The trajectory of the afternoon sun is moving off to his right. "Since the sun sets in the west home must be that way," he says, pointing.

"What if there is a curve?"

Hudson kicks at the relenting soil between the ties. "Find out for yourself."

"What are you going to do?"

"I want to see who those voices belong to. Will you be all right if we split up for a little while?"

Speck chews on the inner part of his cheek. "I think so."

"I won't be long. Let's meet back in an hour."

"I don't have a . . ."

"Use your best judgment." Hudson slides down the slope to the edge of the forest where the trail continues. "Watch the dogs at all times. They know this terrain better than we do. They'll hear a train before you will."

"All right," Speck says, unconvinced.

"You'll be fine. I won't be far."

Before his brother can say anything else, Hudson pushes down the path. Motorcycle tire tracks score the hot dirt in ravines. This side of the railroad shows plenty of signs of occupants—beer bottles and chip bags. Here, Hudson figures, is no longer Muller property.

Not far from the tracks Hudson hears the unmistakable trickle of water. A modest stream weaves in and out of the trees, pacing the trail. Over the sound of the water, Hudson can discern voices before he actually sees a group of people splashing around where the stream widens into a broad pool. On the bank across from Hudson are two ATVs parked side-by-side. A young man is pulling beer out of a cooler. He carries the bottles over to a girl sitting on a blanket sunning in a sliver of light along the shore. A portable radio plays heavy metal music loudly.

Hudson, still unseen, tries to decide what to do here. Three guys and two girls, all about his age or a little older, are splashing around in the water. One of the guys, shoulder-deep, lights a firework with a cigarette and underhands it into the sky. The others watch it rise and then descend. Holding a thumb over the lips of their beers they take shelter beneath the surface. The kid with the cigarette keeps it clutched beneath his teeth as he submerges. The firecracker explodes a few feet over them—the concussion startles birds—and they come up out of the water sputtering and laughing.

Back home, Hudson has mostly managed to remain indistinguishable from the host of other kids his age roaming the high school halls. From time to time football players will hassle him. Once, in the bathroom, just after lunch, a running back made him drink a cup full of used chewing tobacco. It was all he could do to hold it down. He has never mentioned the incident and ignores the assholes who make gagging sounds when they follow him in the hallway, taunting, "I got something else you can choke on." He has convinced himself that he'll fight back if something happens again. He even visited a self-defense website and learned how to bend a man's hand back to the wrist in a way that incapacitates. When he tried it on himself it seemed to work.

Brushing hair from his face and burying his hands in his pockets Hudson steps out to greet the others. "Hey," he says, nodding to the guy with the fireworks. The kid is wearing cut-offs and a bandana over his head. Water drips down his cheekbones. He is sinewy and lean, the muscles in his chest sharply defined—the kind of person capable of getting knocked down more than once.

A shorter, stouter kid responds. "Hey," he says, tugging at his slipping swim trunks as he trudges to Hudson's side of the shore. "Where did you come from?"

The girl in the creek spits a long rope of water in Hudson's direction.

"Turn that down," the guy wearing the bandana shouts to the kid near the radio.

"Nowhere," Hudson says. He stands straight with his legs square.

Attached to a branch on a nearby tree is a rope. The chunky kid swaggers up to Hudson, water dripping, and says, "Nobody's from nowhere. I guess that makes you, Nobody." He flicks water from his fingers into Hudson's face, says, "Bye, bye," grabs the rope and, with a running start, swings out over the water—shorts coming off—and makes an enormous splash next to the girl.

Wishing he stayed hidden, Hudson reluctantly removes his hands from his pockets to wipe the water off his face.

Speck holds his arms out to his sides and walks cautiously down the middle rail. Although the shade from the fir and maple feels refreshing there is no breeze and being exposed on the tracks causes sweat to bead along the boy's neckline. The dogs prance at the forest edge with tongues sagging.

Back home they don't have pets unless you count the fish. His father bought a saltwater tank back when the boy was in first grade. This was something they tended together. Every few weeks Speck's dad took his son to the pet store to buy whatever his son pointed to behind the streaky glass aquariums. To the father, it didn't matter if the fish were compatible with the ones they already owned. The better part of the thrill was in the choosing and the anticipation that Speck expressed, at first, as he clutched the cinched plastic fishbag to his chest on the cab ride back home. When the boy let the fish loose into the tank his father hovered nearby and held his breath hoping there would be peace in the tank for a while. What the father never realized was that his son enjoyed watching the underwater battles. Sometimes at night when he couldn't sleep Speck would stand in the tank-light making combat noises under his breath while the aggressive fish nipped the exhausted, bright, little guys.

Now the tank holds two turtles the father bought Speck's mother for their anniversary.

A glint winking from the forest in the sunlight catches the boy's attention. He investigates. There, half buried in the bushes, is a canteen. Speck holds it to his head and gives it a shake. Inside is nothing. He lets it drop. Deeper in the woods is a scrap of cloth. The boy weaves through the tangles. The dogs overtake him and forge a path for him to follow. Caught up in the low branches of a tree is a camouflaged backpack. This is something someone probably tossed from a train, Speck deduces. He'd like to know why. What makes the most sense is something illegal like drugs or weapons. To his dismay, the pack is empty. Ahead, Sultan has found something.

Leaving the pack dangling in the tree, Speck trudges to the dog. Sultan licks the boy's hand and then runs ahead to catch up with Pepper. On the ground in a bed of poison ivy Speck does not recognize is a black, leather-bound book. He crouches down and opens it, hoping that there is money tucked inside.

The handwriting on the pages is organized beneath a date and time and written in cursive. Speck flips through and no bills flutter out. Before he has a chance to scrutinize any further he hears a whistle. Sliding the book under the waistband of his shorts, Speck retraces his steps back to the tracks.

Hudson takes a deep breath. The locals splashing in the water have turned their attention to him. The couple on the other side by the radio are making out on the blanket. Churning slowly toward Hudson, the guy in the bandana wades ashore. Water drips from the dangling pockets exposed in his cut-off jeans to form puddles of mud in his footfalls.

Not sure what to do with his arms, Hudson folds them.

"What's up?" the guy asks.

"Nothing."

"Got a name?"

"Your friend already gave me one."

The kid in the bandana sniffs violently and rubs at his nose. "My man Bowlie's a clown. He entertains us."

Bowlie dog paddles from the deep blue water in pursuit of the girl standing in the shallows. When he tries to dunk her, she easily elbows him in the gut and then splashes ashore. "Hey, Pike," she says, approaching the guys. She is skinny in her two-piece bikini. "You offer him a beer?"

"Didn't your daddy teach you that you shouldn't offer beer to strangers?" Pike asks. "For all we know Mr. Nobody here just robbed a train." Pike removes his bandana and holds it dramatically over his mouth. "Stick 'em up." With his hands in the shape of guns he pokes at the girl who grabs Hudson to use as a shield. "Stop," she squeals. "I think I stubbed my toe."

Pike tucks the bandana in his pocket, shakes his head, sprints at the rope swing and throws himself at the water. As he dangles, he tries to kick Bowlie in the back of the head. After he makes contact, he spins away and flops flat against the water with a smack.

"Thanks for protecting me," the girl says. "I'm Aubrey, by the way. Never mind those guys."

"Hudson. I don't mind them. How is your toe?"

"What? Oh, that was a lie. I'm fine." Aubrey takes her hands off Hudson's shoulders and pulls them through her long brown hair.

Not sure where to put his eyes, Hudson settles his gaze at her bare feet in the mud.

"Hop in."

"Another time."

Aubrey kicks mud on Hudson's sneakers. "I could get them to throw you in, you know."

"I don't doubt that."

"Chicken," Aubrey playfully pushes Hudson's chest, catching him off guard, and then she too grabs the rope and satellites off the bank, arching over the water before dropping delicately in.

Without thinking it through Hudson unlaces his shoes, unpeels the socks from his feet, wiggles from his jeans, and tugs his shirt over his head with one hand to stand as white as a fish in his boxers. From the water, Aubrey whistles. Bowlie hoots and bobs in the turbulent wake of his own making. The couple on the blanket perks up. Pike smiles and steps out on the other side of the stream on his way to the cooler. "Get a fucking tan, Nobody," he shouts.

"Fetch me a beer, bitch!" Hudson yells back, not himself and loving it. Instead of swinging from the rope, he climbs it, shimmying his way to the weary branch of the old oak. When he is crouched and balancing unsteadily it occurs to him that he could easily fall. *And if I fall, I will break a leg, at best. With a broken leg, I won't be able to go to work tomorrow. If I don't go to work, I won't be able to show dad that I can hold my own. If I can't hold my own, he'll think I'm weak* . . . Pushing the thoughts out of his head and concentrating on the buzz of the others below who are feverish in delight at this turn of events, Hudson hollers loudly and springs out into space.

The train passes slower than Speck expects. He was hoping for the big rush of the locomotive. He wanted to feel a part of that power suck him away and into something new.

What Speck got was a passenger train in no hurry. People at window seats made eye contact with the boy. Some of them nudged their companions so they could share in this discovery together—*Look, a native child!*—pointing and smudging the glass. Before the train was halfway gone Speck took out the pocketknife and carved his name into a telephone pole. Now, as the caboose makes its way along, he slips back into the cover of the forest to hunt for the dogs.

Not far from the tracks is a stream, and that is where he finds Sultan and Pepper sniffing at something in the brush by the shore. When he tries to investigate Speck is surprised to see Sultan bare teeth.

"Whoa, hey," Speck says, backing off. "Have at it, brother."

Pepper, though, is more interested in playing with the boy. He lopes over. "Yeah, I like you much better," the boy says petting the dog's hot white fur. "Let's get you cooled down."

Speck strips off his shirt, sets it with the diary and pocketknife on the bank, and removes his shoes and socks. Stepping cautiously in, he cups handfuls of water over his head and along Pepper's back. The dog wades up to his knees and tries to nip the spray Speck splashes which is when the boy notices split pieces of two-by-fours spiked into an oak on the other shore. The steps lead to a hunter's blind that nestles into a canopy of sturdy branches. If it weren't for the chunks of wood jutting out from the trunk, Speck never would have spotted the blind.

The stream is not deep. The water never reaches higher than his armpits as the boy sloshes across. Pepper hesitates. The dog is undecided, not willing to trust the boy entirely just yet. He stands in that indecision looking from the boy back to Sultan.

Once ashore, Speck tries to shake himself dry. The soft underside of his feet is dotted with red indentations from the rocks. Wrapping his feet around the bottom step awkwardly, Speck tests the strength of the old wood affixed to the tree by a single rusty nail. He decides it will hold. By heaving himself up, Speck grabs a higher step and climbs up the rungs.

The blind is high enough to survey a wide swatch of the stream. Speck has to bend through a clump of leaves in order to pull himself onto the planks of wood built securely around a forked split of thick branches. When he is situated above, the boy takes deep breathes and tries to calm the rattle in his chest. He stands with his legs apart and leans against a chest-high rail that has been built around the perimeter. Up here the air is cooler with a moist, mossy scent. From his vantage, looking in the opposite direction from which he came, Speck can see the top of a house. Upon further investigation, he spies several homes, and they all look new and uninhabited. A person could take a bath in the stream and never know how close they were to civilization. Speck wonders about the hunters who have stood here before. Someone with good aim could snipe a man mowing the lawn at one of the new houses, and the fool wouldn't ever know what hit him. Just mowing along and, *Pow, boom, dead!*. Speck wonders how long the lawnmower would proceed after the dead man let it go. Likely, though, the hunters who stood here before had their eyes trained down below by the stream. The boy extends his right arm and holds it with his left hand up to his cheek, uses the knuckles in his fist as sights, and pretends that he's got a rifle. He swings his arm around slowly until he spies the black German Shepherd still feverishly digging away under the elm. He holds his breath, steadies himself, and, without an ounce of remorse, squeezes the trigger.

When Hudson lands, it hurts. His calves and ass hit water first and will sting all day. The locals are impressed by his spontaneous behavior. Not to be outdone, Pike climbs to a higher branch and throws himself down, wiggling through the air, all bones and bravado.

"You're next, Bowlie," Aubrey says. She splashes him.

Bowlie submerges and torpedoes into deeper water. Pike pops up triumphantly.

"Eight point five," Aubrey shouts.

"Oh, come on. At least . . ." Midsentence, Pike is tugged under the water by Bowlie. When he returns to the surface Pike hits Bowlie in the face with his fist in a way that is not playful but which Bowlie interprets as such, and the two wrestle awkwardly in chest-high water.

"Do you guys do this all the time?" Hudson asks. He takes a quick gulp from his bottle of Molson.

Aubrey sinks low so that her hair floats in a soft net. "It's summer. Our last. Everyone but Bowlie has graduated. That dumbass got suspended for taking the principal's car out for a joyride."

"Intelligent."

"The administrators take advantage of our Auto Mechanic class. Bowlie took Mr. Taylor's Probe for a spin before the oil change."

"He wreck it?"

"No. Speeding ticket."

"Not good."

"Are you done?" Aubrey swipes Hudson's beer and takes a pull.

"Another year," Hudson says.

"Just a pup."

"Give me that back," Hudson says, lunging for the bottle. Aubrey spins away, splashing and kicking. The two tussle and the beer spills, and Aubrey worms away and out onto the shore.

"Here," she says, "take the damn thing."

"So, what are your plans now?" Hudson tries to swallow deeply and ends up choking a little.

"You mean, like for life?"

Hudson wipes his face with the back of his arm and nods, yes.

"College, I guess. Not right away, though. My best friend, Jaime, over there with her boyfriend," Aubrey points, "and I are going to travel to Europe. Our graduation gift."

"I'm jealous. Want some?" Hudson offers the beer.

"Sure."

"Finish it."

"All right," Aubrey drains the beer and holds the empty bottle against her leg. "You meet Maddy yet?"

"Muller? Yeah. You know her?"

"Everyone knows Mad Muller and her mad family."

"Not me."

"Better off not knowing."

Hudson holds his tongue. He can sense how eager Aubrey is to unload the local gossip. He tries to change the subject. "You guys got plans tonight?"

"We'll be here. You should join us."

"Maybe."

"You know, she tried to kill herself recently. Did you notice the bandage on her wrist?"

Hudson hadn't.

"Suicides run in families."

"I don't believe that for a second."

"It's true whether you believe me or not. And I'm telling you that Maddy is damaged. She was there when her grandmother hung herself. Sat there and watched it. Honest. Be careful around her."

"Look," Hudson says, "I've got to go find my brother." He dresses quickly, upset at how easily his mood has shifted. "Thanks for the beer."

"Help me up," Aubrey extends a hand that Hudson grabs. As he's pulling her toward him Aubrey steals a quick kiss on Hudson's cheek before he has a chance to turn away. "There will be plenty more later."

Hudson can't stop a quick flush from rising to his face.

"You leaving, Nobody?" Pike shouts from the water.

"I am."

Pike extends his middle finger.

Hudson waves, reluctantly.

Speck imagines Sultan collapsing gracefully in a heap by the trunk of the tree, a kill shot. Whatever the dog has discovered, he is unrelenting about it. Pepper senses this and keeps his distance.

A quick gust forces Speck to take hold of the plywood. The wind rolls above the stream and back into the forest across from the boy. For a moment the branches of a tree part, and Speck sees another blind. It is tucked away in the elm under which Sultan is flopping around on the ground in whatever mess he has discovered. In that brief moment when the wind exposes the blind, the boy sees movement. Something swift that's gone swiftly. He's sure of it. He freezes and stares. Waiting like this, Speck thinks of time. Surely, an hour has passed. His brother is probably worried by the tracks. It might just be a squirrel, not some deranged old war vet harboring resentment against young boys prying and snooping.

To be on the safe side, Speck hurries down and fords the stream. Pepper is waiting—still caught there in the shallows—and is happy to greet the boy. Speck slides into his socks, shoes, and shirt, tucks the journal back into his waistband and the knife into his sock. Maybe his eyes were playing tricks on him. The tree is *right there*, after all, and he's fine. He has not been sniped or jumped or shouted down. He leans his head closer to take a peek.

Unlike the blind Speck climbed, this one does not have rungs. He is not exactly sure how a person could get up there without being able to climb like a monkey. The blind looks identical to the one across the stream. The hunter probably wanted to cover his bases or else shoot with a friend. Standing cautiously below and peering up, Speck hears a low buzzing sound over the stream before he actually sees what's above. It takes the brain a few moments to comprehend.

Teeming in the branches and covering the whole of the blind are wasps, Speck thinks, or else nasty-looking bees. He's not exactly sure of the differences. The insects are red and black and, even from a distance, big. At first, as he squints, the boy thinks that the hunter has built another rudimentary plank in the branches above the blind. As he scrutinizes he realizes that it is an enormous, flat, nest, nothing like the beehive he discovered in the old outhouse earlier. Now that he's under it, Speck can't believe he hadn't noticed the insects earlier. The entire tree seems to be infested and thrumming.

Speck takes a step backwards and nearly trips over Pepper who has crept up behind him. Stumbling, the boy catches himself with one hand and goes down on a knee. "Whoa, boy, don't sneak up on me like that." Pepper's ears are folded and his tail is creased between his hind legs. Sultan ceases rolling in the mess and, from his back, regards Pepper.

"Hey, it's all right," Speck says, standing. The boy knows better than to touch the dog. Now that he has seen them, Pepper is locked in on the insects.

"All right, boy," Speck says wishing he could muster more authority, "let's just . . ."

Pepper starts barking. The noise is quick and serious, meant to warn. Speck glances up into the tree in time to see hundreds of the insects descend. They are on the dog in an instant. Speck bolts. He sprints to the tracks and covers his head and neck as best as he can. A cloud of wasps pursues the boy stinging the exposed pink of his arms.

Pepper is blanketed—stunned into silence. He staggers, jaws snapping, back into the water. Sultan picks up barking where his brother left off. The wasps turn their attention to the sound and, in platoons, attack the black dog.

Confused and disoriented, Pepper flaps across the water, fending for himself, and shakes off most of his attackers. He darts like a spooked buck through the trees.

5.

Speck breaks from the trees in a blind tear, the wasps still buzzing around his head. Swatting and cursing, he sprints up the slope and onto the railroad tracks. Exposed in heat, the wasps are reluctant to keep after the boy. Instead, as a group, they huddle in the loose dirt beneath the tracks.

Sprinting on railroad ties is impossible. Speck will certainly break an ankle. Noticing the insects have given up the pursuit, he slows to a quick shuffle. On his arms are quarter-sized welts. They are both itchy and painful so that when the boy scratches he feels sharp stabs. He holds his arms to his sides and concentrates on his destination.

Hudson sees his brother hurrying toward him. The boy is flushed and Hudson can sense an air of dissipating panic. When he is close Hudson asks what's wrong.

"I'm never going into the woods again," the boy says, holding his arms out and nearly hyperventilating.

"What happened?"

"I was attacked by bees. Or wasps."

"What did you do to piss them off?"

"Nothing. Pepper started barking, and they swept down. They were huge and very fast."

"All right," Hudson drapes his arms around his brother. "Let's get back."

"I feel a little dizzy."

"You're dehydrated." Hudson turns around and bends low, offering his shoulders. "Piggyback time."

"No way."

"Wrap your arms around my neck . . ."

"Fine," Speck says, embracing his brother.

Though it is difficult and Hudson can feel the strain in his lower back, they return to the house where Madison is waiting on the stoop.

Speck slides off and walks dejectedly up the steps to Madison. Hudson places his hands on his thighs and tries to catch his breath. His shirt is soaked with sweat. The high sun above shows no sign of retreat. If anything, the day has gotten hotter. "Is it eight already?"

Madison is crouching so she can console Speck. "It's seven. I thought I'd ask if you wanted to grab something to eat. What happened?"

"Is my dad around?"

"I was attacked," Speck says, extending his arms.

"Yikes," Madison says. "Are you allergic?"

"I don't know."

"Come on," Madison says, guiding the boy inside. "I'll find some antiseptic."

Hudson follows. He enters the kitchen to get his brother a glass of water. While Madison is in the bathroom rooting around the medicine cabinet, Speck slides the journal he found onto the bookshelf in the den and then slumps into one of the leather chairs. He props his feet upon the coffee table.

"Here," Hudson says, returning. "I'm calling mom to find out if you're allergic."

"No, Hud, don't," Speck says, sitting upright. "This is her vacation. If she thought I was in trouble she'd cancel, you know that. Let's just see if the swelling goes down."

Madison enters the room with rubbing alcohol and cotton swabs. "This is all I can find. It will sting a little," she says, sitting on the arm of the chair next to the boy.

"Thanks," Hudson says. "I can do that."

"It's no problem. And stop thanking me."

"Ah," Speck says, distracted by the quick pain from the alcohol.

"Sorry," Madison says. She blows lightly on the stings. "Is that better?"

The thrill of having her so close nearly outweighs the pain. "It is," Speck says, clenching his teeth.

Madison smiles, catching on. "Do you have a girlfriend back home?"

"Ten," the boy winces.

"One for every year he's been alive," Hudson plays along. "Who knows, maybe in a few months you could be number eleven."

"Oh," Madison says, widening her eyes, "I should be so lucky."

"Don't encourage him," Hudson says, heading to the bathroom to wash his face.

"This hurts," Speck says.

"I know." Madison leans closer to the boy. "Listen," she whispers, "I have a question for you, Mr. Petro."

"Don't call me that."

"All right. What's your real name?"

"Is that your question?"

"Yes." Madison applies alcohol to the welts at the back of his neck.

"Joshua," the boy says reluctantly.

"I like that name."

"What's wrong with Speck?"

"Nothing. I just like Joshua better."

"I hate it."

"What about Josh?"

"Josh is a joke."

"Right. Nicknames can be tough. Some people call me Mad. Would you rather be called that?"

"Angry mad or crazy mad?"

"You choose."

"Well," Speck says, considering. "Neither, really."

Madison screws the top onto the alcohol bottle. "I've discovered it's better to embrace nicknames than to avoid them, Josh."

"All right, Mad," Speck says, scratching his arms. "I'll give it a try. But only from you."

"Fair enough." Madison stands. "Don't do that to your arms. They won't heal. You should rest now."

Hudson enters the den. His face is tight with concern. "How is he?" Not knowing what else to do, he places his wrist on his brother's forehead.

"Better, I think. Probably should rest."

"Good idea. Finish your water."

Speck does as he's told. When Hudson's face is tightened into a cinch the boy knows better than to disobey.

"Do you want me to carry you?"

"No," Speck says when he's done with the water. "I can manage." The boy uses the arms of the chair to help him rise. He is surprised how unsteady he is on his feet and tries hard not to let on as he struggles into the bedroom.

"Thanks, again," Hudson says, turning to Madison.

"What did I say about all this thanking?" Madison slinks into the chair. Her bracelets make a tinny little noise.

"Right. I forgot." Hudson leans a shoulder against the bookshelf. "I'm going to have to take a rain check on tonight. I don't want to leave him."

"I understand."

"You could stay?"

"No," Madison replies. "I'm committed."

Hudson considers bringing up his encounter with Aubrey and the others by the rope swing but thinks better of it. "Some other time, then."

"How were the woods?" Madison asks. She rests her chin on her hands with her elbows on her knees and stares hard at him.

Hudson tilts his head, surprised that she should ask something he was just now thinking. He hates being so transparent. "You didn't follow us, did you?"

"Why would I do that?"

"You wouldn't," Hudson says regaining his composure. "They were fine. We had the dogs. I hope that they're all right. In our hurry to get back we left them behind."

"They'll survive. They own those woods." Madison rises to her feet and stands close to Hudson. "Wasps or bees aren't the worst thing you can encounter back there."

Hudson fights the urge to kiss Madison. The sweet scent of her perfume, her half-parted lips, the innuendo in her luminous blue eyes; they tug like an invitation. Instead of making an advance, he remembers that he is dressed in sweat-drenched clothes and reeks of body odor. Stepping away, he turns his attention to the bookshelf. He sees *Great Expectations* and *Oliver Twist* and says, "These are pretty fantastic, don't you think?" with an escalating lilt in his voice.

"I wouldn't know," Madison says. "They were my grandmother's. She was the reader in the family."

"Right," Hudson says. "I heard about her. I'm sorry for your loss." The moment he has said this he regrets it. And there is no time to recover.

Madison frowns. "From whom?"

"Ah," Hudson responds averting his eyes. He wishes he would have risked the kiss. "I ran into some people by the pond. Audrey, maybe?"

"Aubrey."

"She told me."

"Interesting small talk."

"I'm sorry. I should have told you sooner. When she asked where I was staying I mentioned I was here with my dad and she launched in on . . ."

"It's fine." Madison walks quickly to the front door. "I really need to get going."

"Madison," Hudson says. "I didn't mean to make you angry."

"Oh, I'm not. It's fine." She opens the door to leave. "I hope your brother feels better. Enjoy the show tonight."

Hudson keeps his mouth shut and watches the door close forcefully.

The fireworks commence with a flurry of blooming explosions high over the lake around ten. It is comfortably cool outside, but the mosquitoes are ravenous. Hudson, Clara, Gus, and Nolan are sitting at picnic benches on the front porch of the main house overlooking the water down in the gorge. The air is orange-tinted from the citronella candles Clara has set up along the railing punctuated by cigarette plumes whenever Nolan, and Clara light up. Nolan and Gus are drinking whiskey from squat tumblers, and Clara's holding a glass of chardonnay. Hudson declined the offer to drink tonight. After the awkward glass of wine with his father last night—Hudson had a glass, and Nolan finished the bottle—he has decided to steer clear.

Speck is at the pink house. He hasn't exhibited any life-threatening symptoms. Once he was connected to the Internet the boy spent a few hours looking up the distinction between bees and wasps and then played his video game with online friends. The last time Hudson checked his brother had fallen asleep. The swelling from the stings has gone down. Likely the incident will give Speck nightmares.

For the first time in a long time Hudson notices how quiet it is. The adults aren't saying much—they all seem comfortable enough to simply sit nearby engaged in their private thoughts—and without the sounds of traffic and sirens and shouting that he's used to back home, the world feels fragile. The distant splash of color from the fireworks in the dark sky appears without sound, they are too far away, and this dulls the impact. The night sounds here belong to the cicada and the crickets and the mosquito buzz.

Hudson wonders about Madison at the party. If, back at the railroad this afternoon, he ignored the voices, stayed with his brother, and returned home after a pleasant stroll through the forest, he'd be at the party instead of getting eaten alive and waiting with a cresting anxiety for a grand finale he won't be able to hear. On the other hand, Hudson chastises himself for wanting to be elsewhere. Hasn't he spent countless hours back home anticipating this reunion with his dad? Wasn't this the summer that the two were going to bond? And now he's in a hurry to leave?

"You all right, son?" Nolan asks, cupping his hand over his lighter to get at his cigarette. "Why don't you sit down? You're making me nervous."

"I'm fine. I was thinking I'd check and see if Speck is awake. Maybe he'd like to see the finale."

Nolan mumbles something around his cigarette that only Clara can hear. The woman turns a sympathetic glance toward Hudson and her face, in the candle glow, is an older replica of Madison. The only difference is the eyes; Clara's are not inviting.

"What was that?" Hudson asks.

Nolan smirks at his son. He runs his tongue around his lip and then spits a fleck of tobacco at the ground. "What was what?"

"Nothing," Hudson says. "Nothing, Dad."

"Tell him I've got some M-80s," Gus offers. "We'll blow up a watermelon."

The walk between houses is long enough for Hudson to clear his head. He kicks gravel as he shuffles in the darkness. He wishes he could be more apathetic, just not care one way or another about what the old man thinks. All through his adolescence he imagined a version of his father who left because he felt a calling. He was destined to embark on a quest. His dad, the hero, had dragons to slay and would return—any day now— to tuck his son into bed with an endless supply of adventure stories. Each year the sheets grew shorter. The books piled up on the nightstand.

In the porch light of the pink house Hudson is surprised to see his brother. Speck is standing at the far edge of the stoop against the rail and facing the fields and the forest. The crunch of Hudson's footfalls distracts the boy, and he turns around apprehensively.

"Oh, it's you," Speck says, relaxing.

"You awake?"

"What do you think?"

"Sometimes it's not easy to tell." Hudson takes the steps to the porch and approaches his little brother. He checks on the welts on the boy's arms and neck and decides that they haven't gotten bigger. "Why didn't you join us up at the house?"

"When I woke up and looked out the window I saw something that way," Speck points at the woods. "Light in the trees."

"A UFO?" Hudson teases.

"I'm serious." Speck shifts his weight. "I came out here to try and see clearer."

Hudson peers out. The world is cloaked in darkness. "If you really want to see you have to turn the light out. Funny how to see in the dark you have to be in the dark."

"I didn't want to do that," Speck says quietly.

"Look," Hudson says, "those kids I saw earlier are partying. They're probably running around with flashlights or something. It's no big deal. If we hurry we can still catch the finale. Gus is going to blow up some fruit. It's not great, but it's something. What do you say?"

Speck shrugs.

"I thought you liked fireworks? You were excited earlier."

Hudson can see a ball rise up in his younger brother's throat, and his eyes saturate, frustrated by the outcome of the day. "All right," he says. "Forget them. Let's go inside, and I'll tell you a story."

6.

Bees have hairy bodies. They have round abdomens and wide legs. Bees collect pollen, sip nectar, and drink water. They cluster around flowers and live in hives within which they build a honeycomb. To protect themselves or the hive bees will sting, and when they do they die. The stinger is ripped from the bee's thorax and embedded in the skin. An allergic reaction to the venom in the sting kills, on average, fifty people in the United States every year.

Wasps have smooth bodies. Most of them are predators who feed on caterpillars and flies. They are attracted to human food, soda, beer, and wine. The type of nest a wasp builds depends on its species; some are made out of regurgitated wood pulp while others are constructed with mud. Unlike a bee, wasps are easily provoked and can sometimes be aggressive. The wasp's stinger is smooth and slides easily out of the skin. When a wasp senses danger it releases pheromones to alert the rest of the family who will then join in on the attack.

As soon as it can the sun blankets the fields in an anxious rage and sets to burning away the world. It is not yet seven, and Hudson already feels the ticking sensation that precedes an earnest sweat. He stands with a cup of coffee on the front porch and squints up the wind-eaten dirt path toward the main house. Without meaning to, he wonders what time Madison got in last night.

Back inside, Nolan and Speck are still sleeping. Shortly after Hudson began a story—about an invisible boy who lives on a train—Speck drifted off.

Hudson had retired early himself partly to stay close to Speck and partly to avoid returning to the adults in the post-firework balm slowly soaking into a buzz. Hudson didn't hear his father return to the house last night.

As he drains away the bitter remnants of his coffee Hudson sees a white van pull into the Muller parking lot and then, after first making a small circle, come bending down the dirt road. Ladders have been secured atop the van, and they jostle loosely as the driver negotiates the difficult dirt. Hudson can read the name of a telephone company still showing through the white spray paint the owner used as cover. Trying hard to muster up enthusiasm for the day, Hudson sets his coffee cup on the porch rail and stretches his arms over his head before trotting down to meet the man he'll be working with for the next few weeks.

Through the half-open window, the man looks Hudson up and down and smiles. "There's not much to you, is there?"

Confused, Hudson looks himself over and then glances at the man for some kind of clue. The man has dirty-red hair and eyes an inch apart. His lips are two centipedes. There is an off-center cleft in his chin. "Excuse me?"

"Hop in, Beanpole. We've got a long day."

Hudson frowns. Going to work is something he told his father he would do in order to show the old man he could earn his keep. When Hudson asked his dad if he knew about any summer job opportunities, several weeks ago, Nolan gave Hudson two options: work an ice cream truck in the suburbs or else hang drywall. Without a driver's license, the choice was easy.

Hudson stays put. "Your name is James Crowley, right?"

"Just Crowley," the man says, drumming his thumbs on the steering wheel.

"I'm Hudson. Let's not do the *Beanpole* thing."

Hudson doesn't expect the man to split open his thin-lipped mouth and howl with laughter. When he is finished, a half-minute later, he says, "I meant nothing by it, Hudson. Perhaps you'd deign to join me in our chariot so that we may commence our adventure?"

And this is Hudson's last chance. He can feel it. He can turn around, rouse his brother, hop in the pickup, head to the train station, and be back in the city by dinnertime—just sidestep the generating mess that's brewing. Head down and with a heavy sigh, he shuffles around to the passenger side and slides onto the hot, torn, faux-leather seat. Tools and old wrappers are strewn about the cab, and there is nowhere for Hudson to put his feet except for on a red-and-white-colored cooler. Before he has a chance to settle, Crowley leans forward, swats Hudson's bare thigh, and yanks the cooler out. "Don't put your feet on that, partner," he says and wedges the thing in the seat between them.

"Hudson. It's Hudson. Does this thing have seat belts?"

Crowley chuckles as he spins the van around and up the dirt road. When he is in the Muller parking lot he extends his hand and waves vigorously at the main house. Hudson cranes his head and sees Madison in the tasting room. He is strangely happy to see her up so early. The two of them are prepared to face the day while their parents sleep. His thoughts are interrupted when Crowley leans across his lap so that he can shout out the window. "Hey there, Pixie! How're you healing?"

The look of hatred that Madison sends towards the van makes Hudson shrink into his seat so that there is no mistaking that she is directing it at Crowley. "Get the fuck off me," he says elbowing Crowley.

"That girl, that girl," Crowley says, returning to his seat and pulling onto 89. "May have an angel on her skin, but she's a devil on the inside. I'd jab her with my pitchfork anytime, wouldn't you, Beanpole?"

Hudson shrinks lower into his seat trying to make himself so small he'll disappear.

The boy awakens to discover that he is viciously raking his fingernails up and down his legs. The surprise of his body working away without his permission is replaced by dread as he kicks the sheets aside and inspects the tiny bumps rising like a ridge atop his irritated skin.

His first thought is that the wasps have returned and attacked him in his sleep.

Hurrying to the mirror in the bathroom, Speck finds the rash is faintly decorating his chest. His second thought is that this is a reaction to the stings and, although he knows his brother has already left the house, he returns to his bedroom to look around just in case. Next, he thinks he should call his mother, but this inclination only flares before it fades.

Reluctantly, Speck knocks lightly on Nolan's door. The boy can hear him snoring erratically inside. With a quick peek, Speck sees Nolan twisted in the bed sheets and sleeping with what looks like agony etched across his face. The boy closes the door quietly and backs into the kitchen to think this through. Other than the irresistible urge to scratch himself raw, Speck doesn't feel badly. He does not seem to have a temperature and is levelheaded. He pours himself a glass of water and concentrates on keeping his hands to his sides. Outside the kitchen window the boy sees movement by the barn and thinks of the dogs. But it is not Sultan or Pepper Speck determines as he watches the shadow from the old man spill out across the dirt.

Inside the hangar Gus leans over his canvas and plays his eyes from the landing gear on the plane to the reproduction of it, readying the brush above the paint. On the canvas the rubber tires are bright black and robust. In reality, they are dirty gray and mostly deflated.

"Hey," Speck says, startling the old man.

"Hell, boy," Gus says. "My heart can't take surprise like that anymore."

"Why don't you draw the whole plane?" Speck walks slowly in front of the painting with his arms clasped behind his back like a critic.

Gus sets his brush down. He scrutinizes the boy. Outside, sunlight hangs in the mid-morning. He has an inexplicable urge to dash out into it. Clearing his throat and standing upright he says, "I don't want to miss anything."

Speck runs his fingers along the underside of the Marauder. "It's impossible to get it all. How can you draw the insides? Like *in* the wing?"

"I'll just leave that to the imagination." Gus taps his forehead with his paintbrush.

"Did you fly this actual plane?"

"No."

"Was yours shot down?"

"Yes."

"And you didn't die."

Gus can't suppress a brittle chuckle. He hoists his cane from where it's hooked on the stool. "As far as I know." With effort he hobbles to the side of the plane and stands near Speck. "I didn't actually fly any of the planes. I was a bombardier. My job was to open that hatch," Gus says, pointing to a painting near the barn doors, "and drop bombs."

"Cool."

"Yeah. It was pretty cool when you hit your target."

"You ever miss?"

"You don't want to hear about it."

"I wouldn't ask if I didn't," Speck says quietly as he scratches the rash that's rising up his ankle beyond his socks.

"Don't do that."

"It itches."

"Nobody really listens to me is all I mean. I don't blame them; stories of war are almost always the same."

"How can that be true?"

"The stuff that happens is different, but the way you feel after hearing the story is always the same. Just plain sad." Gus stomps his cane against the ground for emphasis.

"Oh." Speck's not sure what the old man means. Sometimes, the boy knows from interactions with his own grandfather, old people tell you that they don't want to talk about something because they really want to talk about it. "I didn't mean to upset you."

"No, no," Gus says, shaking his head. "It's not you. It's this plane. It takes me back."

"Why don't you get rid of it?"

"I can't do that."

"Does it still fly?" Speck rakes his nails over his skin.

"It could." Gus instinctively scratches his arm. "I told you to stop doing that."

Speck stands straight and slaps his arms to his side. "I'll try."

"All right." Gus takes a deep breath. He taps the worn tip of his cane against the chassis. "I did, once."

"Did what?"

"Miss."

"An accident?"

"We flew in V-formation."

"Like geese."

"Yes. Back then communication was rudimentary at best. My job," Gus motions to the plane and shuffles forward. "I'll show you. Hop up."

The boy eagerly scrambles onto the wing and over to the raised cockpit.

"Slide the pilot's seat back, and you'll see the instrument panel. Beneath that is a handle. Lift it up."

Speck, using both hands and straining, does as he's told.

"Now drop down in there."

The boy climbs in. His voice is muffled, trapped in the small compartment. He scoots forward in the hard-plastic seat. "I feel like I'm in a cocoon."

"Pretty snug. Even for you."

"What's this lever supposed to do?"

"You're in the bombardier's compartment. Now you're the toggler. A bomb dropper. If you pull that lever back to the first notch, you release one bomb. If you pull it all the way back, you release the entire load. Four thousand or more pounds of explosives drop with one firm tug."

"Boom!"

"What you have to do is watch the plane in the lead position—the head goose—and see how many bombs he drops. Everyone does what he does."

"Easy enough."

"Easy enough except for on April 22, 1943 when you're flying lead over Emmerich, Germany, and you're instructed by the pilot over your head to drop a single bomb on your target. Just a peppering to keep them on edge. Easy enough so long as your lever doesn't malfunction—you'll blame it on the damned stick—and you accidentally yank it full throttle and release them all, boom, boom, boom, boom, boom, boom . . ." Gus leans wide-eyed into his cane.

The boy stays still in the hatch.

"The four other Marauders in file emptied their compartments, too. This wasn't a primary target. God knows how many civilians were down there. We—I—blew the town to smithereens." Gus swallows hard and puts a shaky hand to the back of his neck.

Speck isn't sure what he's supposed to do now. He wants to crawl out, and he wants to stay in. The old man said that the war story was supposed to be sad, but he just feels frightened.

The hangar is silent except for Gus's heavy breathing. When he arrived here earlier this morning it was cool enough that he didn't need the fan. With the back of his hand he wipes the spittle off his lips and says, "All right. Get out of there. We should do something about that rash."

By noon, Hudson's arms are rubber. When they first arrived at the new house, Crowley walked around back to the sliding glass door, saying, "I don't get a front door key so we use a rear entry." He slapped Hudson on the back and laughed at this. "That how you take it?"

Hudson bit his lip. All morning the young man has been propping up drywall and holding it in place while Crowley fastens it to the studs. Hudson suspects that Crowley takes his sweet time on purpose when Hudson is holding the walls in position—he whistles and meanders to his toolbox and fiddles around for drywall screws and then adjusts the bits on his drill before strolling over and securing the heavy boards to the studs. All the while Hudson wills his body to stay still and coerces his muscles to obey so that Crowley can't see him shake. Should Crowley see, Hudson knows, he'll make a wiseass comment like he's done all morning.

"You know, Hudson boy, after we get this wall flush I do believe it's time for lunch."

Hudson lets out a sigh of relief and, with his arms splayed against the drywall, he rubs his brow across his already-damp short sleeve. The house they're working is one of two left on the cul-de-sac. Most of the other workers have taken vacations for the holiday, which is why Hudson is able to work without experience. These are modest two story colonial-style homes with four bedrooms and two-and-a-half bathrooms. The Summerfield development abuts the woods and the Muller property. If he wanted to, Hudson figures, he could cut through the forest and return to the pink house. The thought tempts regularly. But there's money to be made, and he's not about to quit. He'd rather sweat through the difficult hours at work than risk looking soft in front of his father.

"What did you bring?" Crowley asks as he drives the final screw.

Hudson let's his arms hang loose. Being inside keeps the sun off but the heat trapped. Drywall dust languidly swirls in the air being circulated by an old, oscillating fan, and it chokes Hudson when he breathes. "I guess I thought we'd go somewhere."

"Oh no, Chief," Crowley says, smiling. "You don't want to throw your money away on fast food."

"What will it take for you to call me Hudson?"

"What are you willing to do?" Crowley winks and blows a kiss.

Hudson sprints to the toolbox, hoists a hammer, and plants the clawed-end into the back of Crowley's neck. The boy kicks sawdust in Crowley's face and then lugs over the bandsaw and begins dismembering in earnest.

At least, that's what he'd like to do. Instead, he says, "Nothing. Just stop."

Crowley turns and walks out to the van. "Monday is liver sandwiches. Mother makes them better than anyone alive. Maybe I'll introduce you to her. You play your cards right she might fix you one, too. I do have an extra bottle of water," Crowley says from the van as he fishes around in the cooler. "You should stay hydrated or you'll have a wicked headache tonight."

Hudson cautiously approaches. He tries to work out the kinks in his shoulders by rolling them in small circles.

In the van, Crowley turns the radio to a rock station and throws back the driver's seat so he can recline and have at the sandwich. "Hey man," he says, "you got any tattoos?" He hands Hudson a lukewarm bottle of water.

Hudson takes a sip. The sun overhead makes his skin feel like wax. With a little energy he walks around to the passenger seat and gets out of the light. "Let me guess, you do?"

"I dabble. Got six so far and am getting another one tomorrow night. By the way, I poisoned that water."

Hudson swallows. He's too exhausted to play Crowley's games anymore.

"I'm just fucking with you. There's no poison in the water, just piss." Crowley chomps a bite of his sandwich and talks with his mouth full. "Anyway, I do a little quid-pro-quo work sometimes at Ink Vein. They got two of the best artists in the state. That's how I know about your girl-friend's tat."

Hudson cuts his eyes at Crowley without moving his head.

"Ah, I got your attention now."

"Madison?"

"I knew her mom way back. Before I got my contractor's license I used to work their fields during harvest. It's hard to work with a hard-on."

"You saw Madison at the tattoo place?"

"Ink Vein. I finished a shingling job recently. That's when I saw her. She wouldn't show me what she'd done."

"Imagine that."

"Can't keep shit from me, though. I know the artists."

"What did she do?"

"Wouldn't you like to know?" Crowley shoves the last of the sandwich into his mouth and chews deliberately, staring at the side of Hudson's face. "I can keep shit from you."

Hudson is momentarily blinded by the refraction of the sun off the van's hood. He holds the half-empty water bottle loosely between his knees. He allows himself a moment to daydream.

"So, what would you get?" Crowley asks.

Hudson considers the question. Getting a tattoo has never crossed his mind. It seems like such a silly thing to do. If Madison really did get one, though, there must have been a reason. Crowley is leaning forward, anticipating Hudson's answer. Ignatius J. Reilly, the protagonist in the book he's reading, is often complaining that he has been spun downwards on the wheel of fortune by the goddess Fortuna. Hudson cringes at the thought of telling Crowley that he'd etch the "Wheel of Fortune" onto his bicep. *Maybe a dunce cap?* Not a chance. Instead, he says, "I'd get a hammer tattooed on my neck so that it looks like the claw-end is puncturing my skin and driving into my brain." Hudson empathetically crumples the empty water bottle and tosses it in Crowley's face. "Let's get back to work."

7.

Wasps belong to one of the largest orders of insects, the Hymenoptera, which means "membrane wing" in Greek. While there are thousands of species of wasp, three common families are the Pompilidae (wasps that primarily prey on spiders), Sphecidae (diggers and mud daubers), and Vespidae (paper wasps, yellow jackets, and hornets). Wasps undergo four stages: egg, larva, pupa, and adult. The average lifespan of a wasp is forty days although female wasps tend to live longer than their male counterparts. The males spend most of their life buzzing around and foraging.

Speck can't quite place the smell in Gus's apartment, and this irritates him. The two walked up the slope from the barn to the pink house under the apexed sun. Then they climbed the stairs slowly. Gus had to take one step at a time leaning aggressively into his cane.

"I'm not going to fall," Gus had said. "But if I did, what would you do?"

Speck stood two steps below, scratching his chest. "What do you mean?"

"Would you jump out of the way or would you catch me?"

"I'd catch you," the boy said, without thought.

Inside, there's a long view over the stretch of the Muller property. An air conditioner in one of the windows hums obediently. A blanket covered in dog fur is heaped beneath the window. In the living room there are stacks of cardboard boxes against the front wall. A sagging recliner slouches against a side table. On the table are a remote, an ashtray, a cigar box, and a large, blue photo album. The television takes up two places at a card table and leaves room for the old man to sit and eat at a folding chair. The kitchen and the bathroom are in the same small doorless alcove—Gus can sit on the toilet and fry eggs at the stove.

"A bit tight in here," Speck says. He cranes his neck to peek into the bedroom. The room is large enough to hold a twin bed, a nightstand upon which Elizabeth's ashes sit in a simple beige urn, and a chest at the foot of the bed.

"I manage." Gus sets his cane on the kitchen counter.

Speck stands in the doorway and keeps his hand on the doorknob so that he doesn't get after his skin like he wants to do. He can identify the cigar smell, the dog odor, the dust, and a hint of grape coming in through the semi-open window. Then there's something else. Like some kind of artificial flower.

"What's that smell?"

"Sit down in that chair."

Speck unfolds the chair by the table and sits. From a cabinet above the toilet Gus finds cotton swabs and calamine and sets them down next to the boy. Then he eases himself into the recliner. "This stuff expired years ago. Better than nothing, right?"

Speck tries to blow a strand of hair away from his eyes.

"Shake the bottle good, pour it onto the cotton ball and dab it wherever you see the rash."

"It's pink."

"Who cares?"

"I'll look stupid."

"Yes, you will. You look stupid with that long hair already."

"I've never been to a barber and I never will."

"Fetch me the scissors in the medicine cabinet. I'll give you a trim."

"I'm supposed to work up at the store today with Madison."

"That's not going to happen. You're contagious."

From the box, Gus withdraws a cigar and a silver-plated lighter. With effort, he stokes it and studies the boy through the puffs of smoke drifting to the back window. "What you smell is perfume. I give the place a good spritz every morning. It bothers the dogs. It's almost gone."

"Oh." Speck begins to shake the bottle vigorously. Then he unscrews the cap and wets the cotton balls with calamine lotion. He applies it like he was told to do. "You ever cut hair?"

"Plenty of times."

"I'm sorry," Speck blurts. This is something he had meant to say earlier. About his wife, about the dogs.

"Fetch the scissors."

"What if you catch what I have?"

"It's poison ivy. A boy your age should know how to avoid it. And a boy your age shouldn't worry about a man my age. My skin is tough like our grapes and just as sour. I'm going to count to three. One . . ."

Speck sets the bottle on the table and walks to the medicine cabinet. The calamine lotion is rapidly hardening, and it makes the boy walk stilted.

"Two . . ." Gus sets the cigar in the ashtray and hoists himself up.

"Here," Speck says. He plops down on the seat and hands the scissors to the old man blades first.

"Boy, you need a lot of work. Lift your chin up and stay still."

Speck tries to sit still. He concentrates on the old man's heavy breathing. Somewhere, a clock is ticking. Every time he starts to shake his knees, he squeezes them together.

"You're going to feel a lot better in this heat after I'm done."

"What's in the boxes?"

"Things I don't want out but can't throw away."

"War stuff?"

"Yes."

"Guns?"

"Don't pry," Gus says loudly and giving Speck's hair a forceful tug.

Speck winces. He has inadvertently struck a chord with the old man. For the first time today he misses his brother. "I'm sorry," he offers, and then closes his eyes.

Gus cuts with abandon. He doesn't stop to think how odd it is that he should find himself in this tiny apartment snipping away at unruly russet-colored locks upon the scalp of an inquisitive boy who seems earnestly interested in his life. He'll think about this later when he's sipping a glass of wine from a bottle of reserve he keeps under the sink and into which he will sprinkle a pinch of Elizabeth's ashes. For now, he minds the ears. He does the best job that he can do. "Done," he says, brushing clumps of hair onto the floor to mingle with dog fur. "Much better."

Speck stands and shakes himself. Several pieces of hair stick to the calamine lotion that makes his skin itch all over again. The boy is suddenly eager to get out of this place. There is nobody in the world who knows where he is at this exact moment, and this thought causes a stab of panic to rise in his throat. "Well, thanks," the boy says. In order to get to the door Speck would have to push around the old man.

"Listen," Gus says, blowing a tuft of hair off his arm. "I don't mean to be gruff. My wife was my better half. Before you go, have a look at that book." Gus nods to the photo album on the coffee table.

Speck realizes that his shoulders have tensed when he sits down in Gus's recliner and hoists the album. He tries to relax as he opens it up. Inside, he is surprised to find butterflies. On each page, under plastic, is a differently patterned, flattened butterfly. "Cool," Speck says, turning the pages. The name of the insect has been written in neat cursive beneath each specimen, and Speck reads them aloud: "Dreamy Duskeywing, Painted Lady, Mourning Cloak, Hackberry Emperor. Who names these things?"

"I don't know. They're drawn to the grapes. My wife fancied herself a lepidopterist."

"How did she catch them?"

"A net, of course."

"How did she kill them?"

Tucked away in the corner of the kitchen is a vacuum. Gus pulls it out and leans against it. "She put them in a padded box so they wouldn't get damaged."

"They'd suffocate?"

Instead of answering, Gus clicks the vacuum on. The sudden noise startles Speck. Here's his chance to make a break. He closes the book and scampers out of the apartment as the old man steadies the vacuum and sucks up the remnants.

Near the end of the workday Crowley and Hudson have hung half of the drywall downstairs. Around four, Hudson collapses from the weight of the walls. The heat, the choking sawdust, the incessant yammering, a lack of food, the purposeful way in which Crowley belches and then blows the putrid liver stench into his face so that he nearly vomits; it all catches up with his body, and he simply lets the sheet of drywall drop and then follows it down to his knees. Crowley, who is fiddling with a bit, is startled. When Hudson says, picking himself up again, he is taking ten minutes and walks outside to the fringe of woods for some fresh air, Crowley doesn't utter a word.

The shade from the trees is five degrees cooler than in the sun and ten degrees cooler than in the house. Hudson can feel the moisture in the air from the thin wind wending through the forest. He envies the people who will buy this house. It is in a fine location. This will be a great yard to grow up in with the trees so close and promising; there's room for a hammock. Someday a husband/father will pound nails into the walls and hang photos of family vacations to the Poconos or Niagara Falls. The husband/father will not be able to really afford the place but will buy it anyway. He'll accept hand-me-downs and get a second job and, tired as a dog from the grind of the day, returning home—here—will make it all worthwhile. Right where Hudson stands now—between the dirt that will someday be grass and the forest—the husband/father will lay on a blanket in the cool of the night with his wife and kids and stare in awe at the vast scattering of stars that goes on forever and ever.

Hudson closes his eyes and pictures it. When he opens them he sees quick white movement in the woods. At first, he thinks this is just sunlight playing off the waving leaves. Then he hears a low whimpering followed by two short yelps. The movement is made manifest when Pepper emerges from the trees with his tail tucked. The dog's fur is covered with brambles, and he gingerly holds one of his hind legs off the ground.

Hudson crouches and offers his up-turned palms. "Hey, Pepper. Are you hurt, boy?" The dog, recognizing his name, hops forward and wags his tail.

"You lost?"

From the house Crowley beckons. Ten minutes have passed.

At the sound of the man's voice Pepper turns back into the woods and barks.

"Probably ought to get that leg checked out."

The dog returns to the woods. He looks over his shoulder as if to say, *Come on.*

"All right. Stay." Hudson heads back to the house. Inside, Crowley has managed to hoist the drywall panel Hudson dropped and secure it in place. He holds his screw gun to his side as if he has just withdrawn it from a holster. Until now it has not occurred to the young man that

Crowley is used to working alone. The kind of strength and endurance it must take.

"If I cut through those woods I'd come out at the Muller vineyard, wouldn't I?"

"Yeah," Crowley says without making eye contact.

"I've got to head back. See you tomorrow."

Hudson waits a full minute for Crowley to respond. The man is a statue. Eventually, Hudson returns to the tree line. He can feel Crowley's disapproving gaze tightening into his back and boring through to incinerate his heart. It isn't until Hudson is with Pepper and they are picking around the brambles that he hears the cackling sound of the screw gun as his boss continues working.

Nolan wakes up disoriented. The bed sheets have been squeezing the life out of him. His mouth opens with difficulty, and there are fireworks exploding in his head. On his way to the bathroom he bumps the nightstand and watches the alarm clock topple to the floor. It is early afternoon. His shift starts in an hour.

In the bathroom Nolan splashes cool water on his face and drinks deeply from the faucet. He opens the medicine cabinet, ignoring his image in the mirror, and palms two aspirin down. Nolan is grateful that pills have always worked for him. His headache will dissipate in twenty-five minutes. He has timed it before.

Stumbling into the kitchen, Nolan opens the refrigerator and pulls bread and bologna out to make a sandwich. He isn't hungry—the thought of food turns his stomach—but he understands the importance of sustenance after a night of drinking. After the fireworks, Nolan, Gus, and Clara stayed out on the porch soaking in the summer humidity. Then the old man turned in. Clara and Nolan held on, waiting for Madison to return. When she did, Nolan said goodnight and walked back to the pink house where he sat alone on the stoop and finished off the bottle of whiskey. He found his bed around the time the sky started to brighten.

When Nolan closes the refrigerator door with his hands full he sees that Speck is sitting on the couch in the den watching him with a book resting in his lap. He nearly drops the loaf of bread.

"Hell, boy." Nolan sets the food on the counter.

"What?" Speck asks.

Nolan considers the kid. "You look different."

"Gus cut my hair."

"How'd that happen?"

"I have poison ivy."

Nolan begins to make his sandwich. He's not used to kid-speak and his brain is moving slower than he'd like. So, he concentrates on the bread and meat and a cup of water from the faucet at the sink. He drinks greedily. Then he fills the cup again. After draining it, he turns back to the boy who has been staring all along. "The pink stuff," he says. "Poison ivy. From the woods. Also, the bee stings. How are you wounds?"

"Wasps. There's a difference. I'm fine."

"I know there's a difference. Try not to scratch the rash. It'll spread."

"I know I'm not supposed to scratch."

"That hair cut makes you look tough."

"It's crooked."

"Would you like a sandwich?"

"I already had one."

"You going to help up at the shop?"

"Can't. Contagious."

"Sweep the distillery. Nobody's down there."

"Sounds thrilling."

"I'm not here to babysit."

"I'm not a baby. I'm not asking you to do anything."

Nolan feels the food trying to crawl back up. His head's still spinning. "At least you have a book."

"Well," Speck says, shifting in his seat. "It's not mine. I found it near the tracks. I think it's somebody's diary."

"Is there a name? Address?"

"I don't know."

"Only one way to find out."

"You think it's all right, then?"

"Sure. There's a reason the writer tossed it." Nolan swallows hard, and this momentarily clears his head. "It's probably some stuff someone needed to get off his chest. It'll bore you to death. No way you'll finish it."

Speck sits forward and scratches his ankle. "Want to bet?"

Nolan spits out a quick, staccato laugh. "What are the terms?"

The boy smiles. "If I finish it, you stop calling me Mr. Petro."

"And if you don't?"

"What do you want?"

Nolan runs a hand across his chin. What he'd like is to reset his life. To go back to the moment he left that crummy apartment in New York City and to grab his wife and child and insist that they brave the future together. What he'd like is for Mr. Petro to not exist. "If you don't finish it, how about you lie to your mother and tell her how much fun you're having here?"

Speck's smile fades. While he doesn't mind lying to his father, he's not particularly good at being dishonest with his mother. She doesn't bite easy. It doesn't really matter though because he's sure that he'll be able to finish the book or else he'll lie to Nolan and say that he did. "Deal, Mr. Baxter," he says, and sticks his hand out for Nolan to shake. The boy prepares to squeeze with all his might.

Hudson can't resist the feeling that he is an actor playing a role in a movie as he follows the white dog through the woods: dog sniffs danger and finds help from a steely eyed young man who charges to the rescue. Likely, though, he thinks, Pepper is just leading him to a patch of wild mushrooms.

Hudson doesn't mind following. It has been such a long day. The job is exhausting, and it won't get easier. Crowley is, perhaps, the most despicable person he has ever met. All day the man has ranted about foreigners, made racial slurs, debased the government, and told crass child molestation jokes. Hearing this hour after hour has taken its toll. It's not that Hudson has been desensitized; he's just been disheartened. There's a small part of Hudson who believes he can get Crowley to come around, maybe enlighten him, posit counter-points, beg to differ. After all, he's just your standard asshole townie. It's not his fault. Now, though, in the canopy of branches and feeling so much less confined, Hudson thinks, *Fuck him.*

Pepper leads Hudson to the little river he swam in yesterday. He's pretty sure the rope swing is around a bend in the water, which means that the railroad tracks are further ahead, and the vineyard is diagonally left. Hudson's happy he's not lost, but he's confused why the dog wouldn't have returned home. Standing on the bank, he contemplates these things. And then he sees what resembles a trash bag tucked into the bushes on the other side of the stream. The dog is staring, too, whimpering and testy.

"That Sultan, boy?"

Pepper folds his ears and barks lowly.

Hudson fords the stream without difficulty. The quick spray cast up from his splashing footfalls feels refreshing. In mid-stride, he cups water and dumps it over his head and neck. Pepper follows behind half-running, half-paddling across. When the dog gets to the other side he hangs along the waterline as if repelled by an invisible force.

The young man strides forward sure that the contorted animal is Sultan. From a distance the dog looks dead. It makes no reaction when Hudson kneels down, but he can see that the animal is breathing shallowly. He is not sure what has happened here, what could have incapacitated the dog like this. Running his fingers across the dog's back Hudson feels that the skin beneath the hot fur is pocked and swollen with a million angry lumps. When it dawns on Hudson that these are stings like the ones upon his brother, he cannot repress a quick prickle of dread from rising at the back of his neck.

The woods are quiet. Pepper is prancing and whining by the water. A two-by-four ladder leads to what looks like a tree house across the stream where he had been standing a moment ago. He'd passed right by it without noticing.

Reluctantly, Hudson looks up. Above, the elm is glistening. Insects, as big as hummingbirds, are crawling over a dozen or more plate-sized nests affixed to multiple branches. To Hudson, they resemble large red-tinted palmetto bugs—he remembers finding one of these "flying cockroaches" in their hotel room at Disneyland several summers ago. The difference is that these bugs are lean with abdomens like bullets, and, even from this distance, he can spot the quivering stinger. Now that he is paying better attention he can hear the unmistakable buzzing noise that accompanies wasps and bees. These, then, attacked Speck and incapacitated Sultan.

The hair on Hudson's arms rises. He instinctively holds his breath and tries to calm himself. He wonders if, like other animals, wasps can sense fear. What he should do, he knows, is run like hell and never look back. Sultan is not his responsibility. He could find help. On the other hand, he is here, right now, in the moment. How can he go for help when he *is* the help Pepper sought out?

Gingerly sliding his arms under the dog, Hudson keeps his head down and sets about the rescue. Now that he has decided what he must do there is no sense in paying any attention to the escalating sound of the wasp noise and the dozen or so scouts who are taking flight to investigate. He does not pay any attention to his aching arms. The dog, as far as Hudson is concerned, is as light as a feather. Here, in his arms, is a garbage bag full of leaves that he has gathered from the make-believe yard he was standing in earlier. He'll just casually walk away. If Pepper is dumb enough to bark and send the insects into a swarm, so be it. He picks through the forest and brushes past the canteen and backpack—the stuff the soldier lost—without noticing. He's sure the railroad is just through a cluster of maple, and he's right. He stumbles into sunlight. Pepper is right behind him. This might be a good place to rest for a moment, maybe set Sultan down and regain his composure, but he decides otherwise. There's still a way to go. Even evening like it is still swelters. The sun in the sky is just pitched at a different angle; the sear is the same.

Sensing the lull, Pepper hurries ahead along the railroad tracks. Hudson is grateful that the animal has taken the lead. All he has to do is keep his head down and make sure that he steps right on each rail and gets out of the way if he hears a train. It's easier on the mind if he counts ties: *one, two, three, four, five, six* . . . Pepper's quick, high-pitched yelping disengages Hudson. The dog is twenty railroad ties ahead and is awkwardly snapping at the air. A cloud-plume of the red-hued wasps has risen from beneath the tracks to dive-bomb the dog.

"Pepper," Hudson hollers angrily, "get over here."

The white dog hunches low and retreats while Hudson carries Sultan away from the tracks and to the tree line on the Muller property. "Let's find a different way home." The young man forges ahead, all instinct and adrenaline.

8.

The smallest insect in the world is a Fairy wasp; it is smaller than an amoeba. Growing up to two inches, the Tarantula Hawk is one of the largest wasps. It takes around 1,500 stings from a yellow jacket to kill a man who is not allergic to the venom. The Cow Killer wasp sting is said to be powerful enough to kill a steer. The Cicada Killer wasp will snatch its prey right out of the air. The Cuckoo wasp produces its own blue-green iridescent light. Horntail wasps attack trees, and Giant Ichneumon wasps attack Horntails. The inseminated female European Beewolf wasp hunts honey bees. To reproduce, Gall wasps don't necessarily need males.

Madison is whisked out of her daydream by the sound of a car horn. Nolan is waving from his pickup truck, on his way to work. Nolan starting his shift means that it's nearly five and time to close the store.

Two gray-haired women wearing pantaloons have been seesawing over two bottles of red table wine for some time. They are the only remaining customers.

"Ladies," Madison says. "I forgot to tell you that today is special. You get two bottles for the price of one. How does that sound?"

The women smile in unison. Madison is taken back by the wide display of crooked teeth.

When they are gone, Madison wipes down the tasting counters like she's done countless times before. She flips the sign to *Closed*, locks the door, straightens the shelves making sure that all the labels are facing outward, puts the few remaining dirty glasses and plates in the dish-washer, sweeps the floor, and places the money from the register in an envelope she'll deliver to her mother.

Madison finds Clara in the kitchen standing by the window and absent-mindedly slicing lemons. This makes Madison nervous. From Clara's posture, Madison can tell that her mother is far away past the vines and through the woods at some tiny speck holding down the horizon.

Just last week Madison discovered her mother standing over the cutting board like she's doing now, slicing away, a discreet pool of blood budding on the floor beneath her feet. Madison couldn't help the shock and surprise that scratched out of her throat and startled her mother. Clara's shoulders hunched protectively, and she clutched the knife and looked with horror first at her daughter hurrying forward and then down at the bloodied cutting board where she had been cutting up a cucumber. Inside that cucumber had been a worm as round as a quarter that had burrowed into the vegetable. It was as big as a small snake. Clara allowed herself one tight-lipped cry before she relaxed her knuckle-white grip on the knife and set it on the counter. She smoothed her bloodied hands along her blue apron and said, "Maddy, be a dear and fetch me a mop."

Now, Madison pretends she has something caught in her throat and coughs.

Without turning Clara say, "Honey, I know you are there. Your bracelets give you away." Madison watches Clara's lips turn up in a smile before she turns her head around to say, "I'm not papier-mâché."

"I just didn't want to startle you."

"I know." Clara uses the knife to hoist lemon slices from the cutting board into a white, plastic, bucket. "How did we do?"

"Not bad, I think." Madison sets the envelope on the kitchen table.

"Do you have any plans for the night?"

"I thought I might go visit the boys. Maybe hunt down the dogs."

"Check on your grandfather, if you don't mind."

"All right," Madison says as she moves towards the door.

"Don't I get a peck?"

Madison stops mid-stride. She had almost gotten away without having to mention the bracelets hiding the bandage at her wrist. "Of course."

Clara sets the knife aside and embraces her daughter. She pushes the hair away from her daughter's face and narrows her eyes. "You are a spitting image," she says.

"I know it."

"I hope you age like her and not me."

"You're still beautiful, Mom."

"We'll see how I look when I turn her age."

"I miss her, too," Madison says.

Clara releases her embrace and, as she does, runs her fingers across the bracelets. "This is a curious fashion?"

Madison tenses. Surely, her mother knows, somehow. It shouldn't be a big deal. There is no real reason why she can't simply yank the bracelets off, rip the bandage away, and show her what she has done. There is no need to explain.

But this is a test, Madison realizes. It's important to hold your ground when pressured, even by her. Madison places a quick kiss on her mother's forehead, spins away, and replies, "It will pass."

Shortly after Nolan leaves Speck uses the bathroom, eats a piece of bread, and returns to the journal on the couch in the den. It smells faintly of the earth. The black cover is fading, and the binding is loose. Nolan's flippant claim that it was thrown from a train bothers the boy. He'd rather pretend that it was purposefully left behind for someone to discover.

Speck wishes he cared about books the way his brother does. Hudson reads all the time. Sometimes, Speck watches Hudson read, and the intensity on his brother's face when he gets enraptured makes the boy envious. Speck has never read anything so engrossing. The novels he has read have been predictable, downright silly, or just sleep inducing. His brother says it's a question of finding the right book. Maybe what he's got in his hands, this battered journal, is it. From what he can tell, the diary is arranged by dates and heading and nothing else. Easing himself into the couch and fighting back the urge to skin his legs, Speck opens the book and reads:

Wednesday, May 15: 22:08

Kylie, I'm going to take your advice and scribble in this journal because I can't stand the idea of you throwing your money away on me. I've been putting it off until now not because I've been busy but because I've been reluctant to allow myself the luxury of missing home.

That's selfish, I know. And I'm tired of stumbling across this stupid thing and feeling badly about not writing in it. The truth is: I miss you. There, now I've gone and written it down. I guess it's something.

"Great," Speck says, "a love story." Then he is distracted by a light knock at the front door. He viciously rakes his nails up and down his leg and is disappointed when he sees pinpricks of blood rising from the crusted pink calamine. Before he can say or do anything the door opens, and Madison pokes her head inside following a loud, "Hello?"

"Hey," Speck says, closing the book. "Come in."

"I hope I didn't interrupt you."

"Not really," the boy says, "just reading."

"You bailed on work this morning." Madison approaches Speck. "How are you feeling?"

The boy shakes his head from side to side. "Not good. The wasp stings are better, but I also got poison ivy." Speck sticks his legs out.

"You're bleeding."

"It's fine."

"Wait here. I'll get a washcloth. You've got to keep it clean or you'll never heal."

While Madison is in the bathroom Speck looks for a suitable place for the diary. Shoving it indiscriminately back on the shelf seems wrong somehow now that he's started it. It needs its own home. On the mantle in the living room are three boxes; one could be big enough. Before he has a chance to investigate, Madison returns with a washcloth. She hands it to him. "I'd do it, but I don't need to catch it from you. I've had it plenty of times."

"It's fine," Speck says, cleaning his legs. The coolness of the cloth temporarily soothes.

"The haircut's nice, too. Your brother did a good job."

"Wasn't him," Speck says. "It was Gus."

"Really?"

"Hey," the boy says, not allowing Madison to pursue the issue further. "What are those boxes on the mantle for?"

"They belong to my grandparents. Well, to 'Gus' now."

"What's in them?"

"I don't know." Madison walks over to the boxes and begins flipping them open. "This one is full of matches," she says as she opens a small, cherry-colored, coffin-shaped box with engraved flowers and a pewter top. "Makes sense over a fireplace."

Speck finishes cleaning his legs and begins reapplying the calamine with cotton balls.

"Ah," Madison says opening a second box that is shaped like a tissue container. "Cigars."

"Do you smoke them?"

"No way."

"What about that big one?"

The largest box is made of walnut. It doesn't entirely fit on the mantle. Madison flips it open. The interior is padded and lined with silky-white fabric. "Empty."

"I think I know what that one was for," Speck says.

"You do?" Madison says. "What?"

"Killing butterflies."

Madison is caught off-guard. She stands with her mouth slightly parted.

"Your grandmother was a lepidopterist, and she put them in there so they wouldn't get damaged. Do you think this will fit?"

"It might." Madison takes the journal from the boy. "My grandfather doesn't normally talk about her."

"Why not?"

"It makes him sad."

"Well I didn't bring it up," Speck says defensively.

"I'm not blaming you. It's actually a good thing. We should talk about things that we've lost. When we remember we stop missing for a while." Madison sets the book in the box. "It's a perfect fit," she says.

"What happens if you find something that someone has lost, and you don't know if they know whether they lost it or not? When do they know to start missing it?"

"I don't know what you mean, Josh," Madison says, leaning against the mantle.

The name sounds like it's for somebody else. Speck shakes his head. "I don't, either," he admits, lowering his fingers to the itch.

Gus corks the urn and stumbles back into the kitchen careful not to drop the bit of his wife he has pinched between his forefinger and thumb. He drops the ash into a glass of Pinot waiting on the counter by the window. The droning air conditioner lulls the old man into a comfortable torpor. He takes a sip of the wine and holds it in his mouth. He is reluctant to swallow—not because the wine is dynamic or flavorful; on the contrary he is frustrated by how bland even this eight-year-old bottle tastes—he'd just like to savor a shared moment with Elizabeth. Gazing out over the fields, he knows what he should do: burn it all to the ground in order to replenish the nutrients in the soil. It's what no other vintner in the region is brave enough to do. There is too much to lose. Tourists and locals alike don't care much about quality. They are lured by the competing names—White Effervescence, Blushing Quintessence, Red Luscious Love, Horny Gorges—with the preposterous labels on the flashy bottles. Wine tasting is something people do in order to tell other people they've done it. He and his wife have spent the better portion of their lives producing the *Muller Roux* with as much integrity and care as the best vintners in France and most idiots couldn't tell the difference between it and a warm mug of grape juice.

The old man swallows the sip bitterly down. "Yes, yes, I know, Elizabeth," he says swirling the glass in the sunlight. "I've got to let it go."

He holds another sip in his mouth and closes his eyes and rests his hip against the vibrating air conditioner and lets time pass. The old man only opens his eyes because he hears one of his dogs barking. He casts his gaze down the dirt road and sees Pepper running awkwardly—limp-sprinting—away from the forest. After a moment, Gus watches Hudson break from the trees hoisting what resembles a half-stuffed garbage bag.

Hudson only realizes that he has been quietly humming "Stars and Stripes Forever," to soothe Sultan, after he has skirted the electrified deer fence and notices Madison rushing down from the pink house. There's a flush of crimson concern stretched across her high cheekbones, and all at once he feels as if the long day might be winding down.

"Is he dead?" Madison slides next to Hudson.

Madison carries in her hair a hint of vanilla. Her sweet scent quickly reminds Hudson how badly he must smell, again. He tightens his grip on the dog determined to finish the rescue. "I don't think so. You better call a vet, though."

9.

Although it is late, the sun is still out directing the vine's shadows in a pantomime. Madison is leading Hudson around a small vegetable garden—cucumbers, tomatoes, green peppers—down a slope between the pink house and the grapes. Sultan is upstairs in the apartment with Clara and Gus. The veterinarian has come and gone. He brought balm for the stings and gave the animal a shot for the inflammation. At the door, as he was leaving, he met Gus's gaze and said, "If you don't see improvement in a day, give me a call. We won't want him to suffer."

Speck is in the hangar, given permission, and Pepper lolls nearby in the dirt with a bandage wrapped tightly around his foreleg.

Hudson has had a hot shower and food. He called his father, who didn't answer, and the young man decided not to leave a message. When Madison came to the door to offer thanks and ask if he wanted to see something cool he tried to act casual when he responded, "Sure."

Once they are around the garden and nearly to the first of the rows Madison puts her hand on Hudson's arm and says, "Here we are."

Hudson looks around. There's a soft breeze rolling along keeping the heat moderate. The ground is dirt and half-grass. "Yeah, this is pretty cool," he says, sarcastically.

Madison squeezes his bicep—Hudson instinctively flexes—and points at a patch of earth in front of them. With her shoe, she kicks dirt away and reveals wood. "Help me," she says.

Curious, Hudson starts to brush the soil away until a large wooden circle—the cover of an enormous barrel of wine—is exposed. It sits atop a slight concrete lip.

"A well?" Hudson asks. He scratches his nose with the backside of his hand.

"Let's open it."

Together, they trace the side of the barrel-top and, with effort, pry it away from the hardened dirt enough to peer inside. Inside is pitch black releasing cool and musty trapped air.

Madison props her arms behind her, sitting comfortably in a tuft of clover, and watches Hudson investigate.

"Looks like there's a ladder hooked inside."

"Here." Reaching into her jeans pocket Madison flips Hudson her lighter.

The thin light plunges a few feet into the darkness and doesn't illuminate much. Hudson scoots over to recline next to her. "The old wine cellar."

"Used to be. My grandfather converted it to bomb shelter. There's more concrete down there than you can imagine."

"You're right. That is cool."

"You can climb down there and follow the tunnel all the way back to the house. There's a hatch in the floor in the den. It was a great place to explore when I was a kid. I could sneak up on my grandparents and eavesdrop."

"Want to go down there now?" Hudson suggests.

"No way. As far as I know nobody has been in it for years. It's home to spiders, snakes, and mice now. Besides, how do I know you would behave yourself?"

Hudson grins. While he doesn't have much experience with girls even he can recognize this invitation. He slides closer, pretending to attack, and tickles her. The two tussle on the ground, laughing and flailing. They end up next to each other, flat on their backs, panting. Above the sky is as wide as Hudson has ever seen it.

Madison reaches over to pick a piece of grass out of Hudson's hair, the bracelets on her arm shifting softly. "It was nice what you did."

"So strange how Pepper materialized like that."

"He recognized your scent."

"You saying I smell?"

Madison tugs his hair. "Just take the compliment," she says. "I don't go around giving them away."

"Seriously, though, I hope the dog makes it. You guys have some badass wasps around here."

Madison rises up on her elbows. "It's weird," she says. "Sultan has come home injured before, though. He's too aggressive for his own good. My grandfather will take care of him." She reaches in her back pocket for a pack of cigarettes. "You mind if I smoke?"

"No."

Madison places a cigarette in her mouth and waits patiently. When Hudson doesn't make a move, she says, "You have my lighter, bright boy."

Hudson strains to sit up. The soreness in his body is making itself known. He produces the lighter and tries to strike it, but his hands are fumbling, and he's nervous, and it takes a few times to get right.

Madison notices. Once the cigarette is lit, she takes his hand in hers and holds it. "How was work?"

"Terrible." With his free hand, Hudson fingers the bracelets. "You know that guy, Crowley?"

"Everybody knows everybody around here."

"Listen," Hudson says, turning to face Madison and speaking in a rush, "I don't want to repeat the same mistake that I made yesterday. Crowley started talking about tattoos, and he said that he saw you getting one done. But he didn't tell me what it was, and I didn't ask. I just wanted you to know."

Madison blows smoke out of the side of her mouth. She finds and keeps Hudson's eyes. Just like that, the out-of-towner is part of the town. It's something she will have to accept. Without warning, she leans forward and kisses him. When she's done, she leans back and says, "Thank you."

Hudson tries to maintain his composure. The kiss was unexpected, but the desire for more is not. He doesn't trust what his lips might say now so he keeps his mouth shut.

"That was nice," Madison says, after a while. She finishes the cigarette. Nobody notices the sun is down. "Hey," she says, scooting forward for another kiss, "come here."

Hudson eagerly acquiesces. Their teeth touch, and he isn't sure just how to chase her tongue with his, but there's a thrill in figuring it out. Hudson uses his weight to guide Madison back to the ground where they can go about the business of making out more comfortably. His hands roam, and his heart catapults.

With the journal Speck sprawls under the wing of the Marauder. The filtered sunlight illuminates the lazy dust clouds descending. He stretches his legs as far away from his fingernails as possible. Just outside the door the white shepherd eagerly looks on. Pepper knows he's not allowed inside without an invitation. So, he pleads with his eyes and occasionally whines.

Speck is not interested in disciplining and wouldn't mind the company. He's surprised how quickly he's come to like the thing. "Come here, Pep . . ."

Before he can finish, the dog stands up and limps across the dirt-hardened floor to nuzzle the boy's neck. "All right. But you've got to behave," Speck says. "We've already gotten into enough trouble in the woods. I'm sorry that I abandoned you back there. You're a good dog for staying by your brother's side. He's going to get better. Sit here."

Pepper curls to the ground and allows Speck to use him as a pillow. The dog licks the boy's ear. Smiling, Speck flips the journal open to where he left off and reads, hoping that the book is not about love:

I've grown accustomed to this place, and that is not a good thing. People here are hard and distant and already a little dead. There's a routine locals follow, and they simply don't stray from it. In the morning, they say their prayers. Then they do chores like wash clay pots, clean haggard clothes, gather wood, tend to the sparse garden, and feed the emaciated farm animals a handful of seeds. Lunch is goat milk and rubbery bread. Then more prayers. Afternoons are spent like the mornings except with different jobs like patching holes in the thatched huts, sweeping the dirt roads, or butchering an animal. Dinner is more bread, sometimes-dried meat, and a cup of milk. Evenings are spent in the mosque. Then it's dark. That's it. Day in and day out. What's curious to me is how expressionless everyone is. There is almost no sign of emotion. Occasionally I'll hear an outburst when there's a brief argument, but that's it. I don't believe I've ever heard them laugh. This, of course, is easy to contrast with the other men stationed here with me. They laugh often and without any reason except to keep the morale up.

We too have a routine in Nuristan. Our orders are to police and blend. I can't get more specific than that, really. When Captain saw me writing in this thing he told me exercise caution. Everything I write will be screened before I can be discharged. And I hope that's soon. *Anyway, we have a routine, too. Where I am is nothing like where I was last stationed. Here, it's wooded and warm. There's oak, holly, and pine. Poachers from neighboring Pakistan come to clear-cut the Himalayan cedar. It's a big business, and there are competing parties of rogue tribes who vie for the richest groves in the forest. We don't get too involved with the skirmishes. Our presence has pushed them down around the border, and we've established perimeters. So long as nobody breeches the boundaries, we haven't advanced. We've been here six months. Locals have gotten to know us and, I daresay, they seem to appreciate us being here.*

But we're here for other reasons, which have only recently been clarified to me. I wish I didn't know what our mission was because it means that I will have to extend my stay over here. My hope all along was to be home for your birthday, but that's just not going to happen. I live on military time, unfortunately, and it doesn't bend to anyone. Not that I'm not owed a break. I've been a good soldier. I keep my head down and do what I'm told.

For now, I'm going to sign off. Over and out. I've got some packing to do. At daybreak I'll be off. There's a good part of me that's excited.

Sunday, May 19: 20:30

I've got a little time to return to this thing. My watch just ended and now Tolly is on patrol. Right now I'm in a lean-to. It's basically a tree house like the ones I used to make with the neighborhood kids only this one is covered with a camouflage tarp. Unless we're dumb enough to make noise or some fool decides to chop our tree down, nobody would ever know we were here. Oh, and unlike Rochester, this place is jungle-hot and prone to monsoons, which are just wicked unrelenting rainstorms. We've recently entered monsoon season, and that's part of the reason we were dispatched here now.

I'll try to fill you in on what I can. We came to Nuristan to ward off some of the tree pirates, yes, but we're also here because our intelligence suggests that certain high-level bad guys on our "most wanted" list use the cover of this dense forest and the chaos of the poachers as smokescreen. They can easily hideout here and then crawl back into southern Pakistan without getting detected. Or, so we think they think. We've plotted out an area of forest that they will have to pass

*through once the rains come—an area of about ten square miles—
and a small platoon of us are expected to terminate them.*

*There are twelve of us total. We're each paired off—sharpshooter
with tracker—in our own section of a perimeter that surrounds a
high stretch of land that won't flood. Presumably, the rats will climb
out of their caves and seek high ground. Getting here was difficult, to
say the least. Climbing the slopes and negotiating the ravines is one
thing but add to that the landmines and booby traps, and you've got
yourself some tricky business. That's why we have trackers. And that's
why I'm still in one piece. I've been paired up with a skinny redhead
named Len Tolly. Just like me, his second tour has been extended.
The higher-ups figure we could sit around and bitch about it, and it
wouldn't lower our morale any lower than it already is. For that reason, Tolly and I swore that we wouldn't complain at all.*

*Looking back on what I just wrote it occurs to me that I might give
you cause for concern. It's not as dangerous as it sounds. And, now
that I've thought about it, I probably won't be sending this journal to
you anyway. I'll just hand it to you when I get home so you'll know
that I made it out all right.*

*Hey, here's something crazy: as we were setting off this morning I
saw this kid—maybe ten or eleven years old—streaking through the
woods in nothing more than a pair of ratty shorts. He scaled a tree
and went swinging from branch to branch over a five hundred foot
ravine. Kid had no fear. On the contrary, you should have seen the
enormous smile plastered on his face. Made me laugh honest.*

*Well, I've got to get some rest so I'll cut this short. It seems to me
the best way to write is to stop when you still have something left to
say so that you don't dread getting back to it. I just hope I don't forget
what I was going to say.*

*One last thing: the mosquitoes here are as big as swallows! There's
something in my blood that makes them swarm around me and, for
the most part, they leave Tolly alone. Knowing this, he tries to stay
close by my side. A real friend . . .*

Pepper shifts, stretches, and stands. Speck sits up and closes the book.
In the short time he has been reading the world seems to have changed
around him. The barn feels smaller, and the underside of the airplane

wing looks vast. The blades of the two propellers catch the last rays of sunlight and yearn to spin.

Speck shoos the dog outside and closes the hangar doors. In the twilight the boy can see his brother and Madison near the garden. From a distance their bodies seem blacked-out and enmeshed.

"Let's get back to the house," he says to the dog as he turns to ascend the slight incline. Pepper's got his ears perked and eyes toward the woods expectantly. Speck wonders if something sinister is about to burst from the trees and attack them. He peers hard, trying to see what the dog senses. For an instant, like a quick wink, a light breaks through. Right about the time that the boy thinks this was just his imagination it comes again, the same light that he saw last night; it has returned. Then he feels as much as he hears the faint, low, churning of a machine.

"A train," Speck sighs. "Of course."

The vibration running along the tracks disrupts the wasps long before the Amtrak train arrives. They are irritated every time a train passes. These tiny insects don't seem to stand a chance against the goliath machines.

Since leaving the main hive in the forest the drones have fastidiously been forming this modest, man-hole-sized nest beneath the rail. Here is not a good location, and the wasps understand this. A dozen of the biggest workers—the knights—carry a tiny queen affixed to the underside of their carapaces. The queens, two millimeter assassins, have paddle-shaped wings meant more for burrowing than for flying. Unlike the bigger red-hued workers, the matriarchs have a translucent body (as flexible as a millipede) capable of changing color to blend with the environment. The queens hang on to their steeds by biting into the thorax. The workers don't mind; they do what's required to propagate the species.

Ahead, in the light beam, the conductor sees what looks like a camp of bats hovering. He squints as he leans forward and then the train plunges headlong.

Most of the wasps disperse and then bounce against the passenger cars. Several windows are wide letting in the cool evening air and into them buzz the determined insects. Once inside, minor chaos erupts. Many passengers have just finished dinner and are preparing to doze. The workers angle toward the heads of the unsuspecting. There are not enough wasps to swarm and incapacitate. This is not the kind of battle the workers will win. A few brave men roll up newspapers and magazines and popular hard-backed books and swat the wasps into a position to crush.

And while the brief, terrorizing five minutes of distraction on the train causes baffled travelers to shake their heads in wonder, and several victims are treated by the on-board nurse for the minor stings on their arms, this incident will not be merely anecdotal—*You're not going to believe what happened on the train ride*—because one of the workers made good. All the stinging and buzzing is a distraction. To fell the giant simply takes a single, Q-tip-sized queen that, during the melee, dropped down onto a shirt collar. The queen will wait for Andrea Davis to fall asleep. Andy is on her way from Brooklyn to Buffalo where she will rent a car and drive north for a clandestine rendezvous in Niagara Falls with a man she met on an online dating service. This is her first visit to the falls, but the man she's meeting has been there many times. Andy will drift off into her train dreams. There is no way for her to understand what will happen next. The queen will climb carefully through the netting of hair and, leading with soft, unassuming, anesthetic bites, nestle into her ear canal and deposit what looks like a teaspoonful of tapioca pudding. The egg sac contains high levels of hydrofluoric acid that burns through the earwax so that it slides through the inner ear canal. Soon, it will penetrate the eardrum and begin the slow burn through the cochlea to the vestibular nerve. In less than a day, the larvae—a half-dozen or more—will squirm out of the sac and squeeze through a tiny hole in the temporal bone that the acid has eaten away. The head is an incubator filled with more than enough protein upon which the insects will ravenously feast. Then the adolescent wasps will burrow into the Eustachian tube and emerge as adults from the host through the nose or mouth.

Before that, the queen will climb back out and die satisfied in the tracking along the windowpane. Andy will momentarily wake up when the queen scuttles out. She will scratch her neck thoughtlessly and then slip into a nightmare.

10.

The world is brighter in the morning when Hudson opens his eyes, and he feels good even with his aching muscles. The first thing he does is check on his brother who slept deeply last night. Speck drifted off wearing earplugs and listening to classical music. *Perhaps*, Hudson hopes, *it helps.*

Lifting the covers away from his brother Hudson can see the rash has spread all over Speck's bare chest. Madison mentioned that there's nothing you can do about poison ivy except wait for it to go away and fight the urge to scratch it. Before leaving the room, Hudson gently applies a coating of calamine without waking the boy.

Peeking in, Hudson sees his father balled up in his sheets, snoring as if in agony. The room is pungent with his heavy alcohol-laced sweat. Hudson pours Nolan a glass of water from the bathroom faucet and sets it on the nightstand by the bed. Then he packs himself a lunch with an extra bottle of water.

When Crowley arrives early, Hudson is prepared. For every ignorant comment the man makes, Hudson smiles or else ignores. He has decided that he will respond to the son-of-a bitch with clipped and vague non-committal phrases. When Crowley takes his sweet time to fetch tools and leaves Hudson struggling to keep the drywall up, he simply sets it on the floor and waits. And when Crowley announces that they're going to take lunch break at 11:30, Hudson says, "All right."

The only space left to hang drywall downstairs is in the small foyer.

As they are climbing into the van Crowley says, averting his eyes, "Listen, I want you to swing by my place. There's something I need to grab."

Hudson doesn't like this one bit.

"Relax. I got to check on my mom," Crowley says. "She isn't feeling well. It's not far."

"I'll just stay here."

"I can't do that. I'm liable."

"You think I'll steal something?"

"No, I trust you. You trust me now."

The older section of the Summerfield development, near the entrance and exit, is teeming with kids playing kickball in the street or else leaping rainbow sprinklers in the brittle lawns. From the passenger seat Hudson admires them. He'd like to get Speck over here. His brother's antisocial tendencies could use some attention. Hudson knows that he is partly to blame for his brother's introversion; given the choice he'd have his head in a book and let the rest of the world fall away. But this is the summer of action without reflection, and whether he likes it or not, Speck is going to have to crawl out of his shell.

"I almost took a job selling ice cream," Hudson says, absently, as they pull out of the development.

"It will make your hands sticky." Crowley smiles as big as his thin lips allow. "Such delicious treats."

Hudson is not sure how to respond so he changes the subject. "You get that tattoo?"

"Took until one in the morning. I'll show it to you soon."

"No hurry," Hudson replies. He eats his lunch as they drive.

Once they are around the lake, Crowley navigates two-lane county roads. "Hey," he says, "if masturbating is so dirty why does cum smell like bleach?"

Hudson has to fight not to choke on his food. He sets his sandwich down, his appetite gone, and concentrates on the world passing by outside the window. Soon, they arrive at the trailer park. An aluminum sign that has suffered a shotgun blast has the word *Lakeview* printed on it. Crowley pulls off the pavement and onto the gravel road. "You know your dad works for the company who manufactures these homes?"

Hudson does not.

"I see him down at Moonshadows all the time."

"I hate that song."

"What song?"

"Nothing."

"It's a bar," Crowley says. "That's all." He pulls into the short driveway. Crowley's doublewide dominates the tiny parcel of land it sits horizontally upon, and it is crammed next to two other homes. Behind the home are train tracks. Hudson wonders if they are the same ones that run behind the vineyard. There's a wheelchair shoved against the side of the trailer beneath a dilapidated carport. Leading to the front door is a sloped ramp made from two-by-fours. The wood has been stained walnut brown, and the railing is painted off-white.

Gravel crunches as the van pulls in, and Crowley kills the engine. Behind Crowley's trailer and on the other side of the tracks is another trailer park. Homes on the other side look in worse condition than the ones in Lakeview. One is festooned with old license plates from a dozen or more states. An orange-mottled mutt chained to a railroad spike gnaws aggressively at its foreleg. Atop many of the structures rickety television antennas claw at a low bank of clouds approaching. Bent aluminum siding shows rust stains, and the whole place oozes a kind of desperation that makes Hudson's bones ache worse than his muscles. Deciding to just get it over with Hudson exits the van and approaches the front door. Crowley makes him wipe his shoes on the tattered rattan welcome mat.

Inside, Hudson is greeted by heavy lilac-scented perfume. The scent is packed into the home and eager to escape. Hudson holds his breath until his eyes water as they step inside. "Might want to open a window," he suggests.

"Mom makes me keep them locked when I'm away. She's afraid of thieves. All kinds of trash blows over from the other side of the tracks." Crowley points a calloused finger at a single door along a wall that runs the length of the trailer set in the exact same spot as the one they've just entered. "Mom's in there." Hudson can see that the builders simply took two identical homes and mashed them together.

Crowley quickly sidles next to Hudson and drapes an arm like a vice around his shoulders. "Her mind is going," he whispers. "She's all paranoid. Thinks we've got mice. Which we don't," he says loudly at the wall. "She won't let me in there anymore. It's locked and bolted from her side. There are bars across her windows. A regular Fort Knox. I have no idea what she does all day other than watch television or the trains pass."

"Why don't you take her to dinner or something?"

"That's not how it works, Beanpole. She takes care of me, not vice versa. At least until she keels over."

"How would you even know something was wrong?"

"The smell, I guess," Crowley says. "I haven't given it much thought. Anyway," he pounds on the door, "there's something I need to get from her place. You're going to help me."

"Me?"

"Sweetie Pie, we've got a visitor," Crowley shouts in singsong. "I've brought a friend. He looks just like Gabriel. Come have a look-see." To Hudson he says, "Say something to Sweetie Pie."

"Who's Gabriel?"

"My dead brother. Fell through the ice. Freak accident. Don't bring it up around Sweetie Pie. Technically he was my half-brother. All frozen, though."

Hudson tries to swallow down his shock.

"Tell her you're here to taste her yummy cookies. Gabe loved that shit."

"I don't want to say that."

"We're not leaving until I get in there. I can wait forever. This is my home."

Hudson scopes the place. He is surprised how quickly he has forgotten the perfumed smell. Off to one side of the trailer he can see a tidy kitchen and a bathroom. To the other side is a small living room with a television, a recliner, a TV tray, and a closed door that leads to the bedroom, he presumes. There's nothing spectacular about the place and at the same time Hudson can't suppress a sickening knot rising up from his gut to lodge in his throat. He wonders, momentarily, where Mr. Crowley is. He knows better than to ask. Shaking Crowley's arm away he stands close to the door. He can't hear anyone on the other side, but he senses someone leaning against the handle. "Ms. Crowley," he says, evenly, "are you all right?"

For a minute nothing happens. Crowley is crouching forward in anticipation. When Hudson hears the deadbolt slide, and the handle begins to turn, Crowley elbows past the boy, seizes the handle and throws the door wide nearly toppling the old woman onto the linoleum floor. Before Hudson or the mother can recover, Crowley shoves into the other trailer and is heading deliberately toward the bedroom. "Hey, Mom," he says, "miss me?"

Ms. Crowley has collapsed to a knee and is in the process of sliding completely to the floor. Her hair is mussed—gray and in tangled curls—and her pudgy, huffing, water-bloated jowls are stained with pink rouge. Her wet, vein-addled eyes are set deeply into her face and regard Hudson with horror. The young man can't be sure if he hears the words "Help me," issuing from her papery-thin lipsticked lips. Her faded, rose-colored smock is wrinkled and stained pea-green around the collar, and as she begins to splay it bunches around her knees.

"Lend her a hand, would you," Crowley says from the other room. "Should be a walker nearby."

The old woman doesn't weigh much, and she uses all her strength to help Hudson lead her over to a dusty couch against the back wall. When Hudson has done his best to smooth her out and let her catch her breath, he kneels down by her side. The look of terror etched into her eyes does not abate.

"Do you want me to get you a glass of water?"

The old woman remains frozen.

"Did I hear you say you wanted help?"

"Poison," the woman suddenly sputters sending a wet spray of spittle into Hudson's face.

"Excuse me," Hudson says, leaning back and wiping his face with his hand.

"My son," she screeches.

Before Hudson can say anything else Crowley enters the room. He grabs the young man by an arm and leads him into the bedroom. "I told you," he says bluntly to his mother. "Come check out Sweetie Pie's pride and joy."

Hudson is half-dragged into the back room. The space has an unmade bed, a nightstand with a crooked shade over a lamp, and a sizeable hutch Crowley is secretively opening. He positions his back to the door and uses Hudson as a shield to block Ms. Crowley's view.

Through the streaked panels of glass in the teak hutch are dozens of tiny porcelain and glass animals packed together and facing forward. Light from two bulbs mounted to the sides of the hutch bathe the figurines in a sick, dull glow. Crowley quickly snatches an animal—Hudson can't see what it is—slips it into his pocket, and softly closes the door. "Look at the little zoo she's got," Crowley whispers. "The halfie and me started buying them for her when we were kids. Whenever a holiday or birthday came around we'd go antiquing in Farmington. Must be fifty or more. Mom knows the precise count."

"A glass menagerie."

"A what?"

"Menagerie," Hudson repeats, reluctantly.

"They're glass animals. Fuck *menagerie*. I've dealt with shit like that all my life." Crowley shoves around Hudson and strides out the door. Hudson is suddenly aware of a trickle of sweat beaded on his nose. The eye-level animals—a lizard, rabbit, skunk, dolphin, pig, rooster—wait to see what Hudson will do. He wipes the sweat away. Then he moves into the other room where he finds Ms. Crowley trying to bar the exit.

"Wait a second, I'm still in here."

"No, no, no," she says, as Hudson pries her away. She scratches his face and clutches his arm. "Please don't let him take any more away. They are all I have left of my angel."

"I'm sorry," Hudson says shaking free and stumbling backwards. He slips through the trailer to the front porch and the daylight.

Sunlight from a crack in the blinds falls directly across Speck's eyes, and he wakes up annoyed. His mouth is dry, the wasp stings throb with pain, and the poison ivy is spreading. He yanks the earplugs from his ears and struggles to his feet. He's got to use the bathroom. When he pushes the door open he is startled by Nolan slumped over the sink, arms holding his body erect, staring into the mirror at his bloodshot eyes and sallow, unshaven face. His mouth is a horizontal line he doesn't bother moving when he sees Speck reflected back in the glass.

"I didn't know you were in here," the boy apologizes, hurrying out of the bathroom and retreating.

In the kitchen, he fills a cup with water and drinks it quickly. His eyes wander to the living room and the boxes on the mantle. After a furtive glance toward the bathroom door, Speck fetches the journal from the padded box and hurries back to his room to settle under the covers of his bed. Anxious for the distraction he picks up where he left off:

Tuesday, May 21: 12:45

I've got a few minutes before I'm off. I finished up my MRE and am under the tarp. It's raining. The rain and wind started shortly after my last entry, and it's been falling ever since. The mosquitoes seem to be multiplying. I'm pretty sure one bit me in the eyeball! And that's not even the worst of it. It's the mud. It's everywhere, and it smells like rotten eggs. Remember the time you found an Easter egg behind the couch that mom had hidden there the year before? Think of that smell, only nastier. When you walk, the ground tugs at your boots like quicksand. More like quickmud. It's eager to pull me into an early grave.

To help you better understand what I do here I'll try to describe it. In the morning, Tolly and I patrol our area, which is about two miles in diameter. I stay behind Tolly who makes sure we don't step in the shit. He's pretty sure that where we are is too dense and hasn't been traveled much. He hasn't detected any signs of humans. After our morning patrol we return to our "base" and check in with the Captain. We report what we've seen which is nothing. Then maybe we'll play a quick game of cards or else just talk. Next is our afternoon patrol in a different direction from our morning sortie. We're back to camp by early evening. Often, I'll take my rifle up to a blind I've made high up where I'll sit like a statue, ignoring the desire to scratch the mosquito bites down to the bone, and wait for anything to move. I've got an infrared scope I can use to keep an eye out in the dark. I'll sit perched like that for as long as I can before I hear Tolly snoring like a truck down below. When it's too loud I have to climb down and shake him awake.

So far, we haven't seen squat. From our correspondence with the rest of the team, they've not seen dick, too. So it goes.

I'm pretty sure you'd like Tolly. He's high-octane like you. His first name is Len, I might have mentioned, but everybody calls everyone else by their last names. Tolly's super-smart. He is from New York City, but he knows everything there is to know about plants and animals—flora and fauna. Told me that growing up in the city made him better appreciate nature. He's a National Geographic *junkie. Learned to track in Central Park. Apparently, he followed people all the time without ever being detected. He claims disappearing is an art. Once he even tracked a mugger stalking a couple and thwarted the attack. A damned superhero!*

Like you, he's got a great memory. Unlike you, he loves football.

He can tell you nearly every play of every game that the Jets made for the past three years. Hell, he could be making a lot of it up, but I don't mind. It's not a bad way to pass time listening to him march the players up and down the field with a lot of enthusiasm.

I do miss football and baseball. Sometimes we toss a canteen around! Pretty pathetic, huh? I'm probably getting a little frayed along the edges. Writing in this thing is good if I want to get things off my chest, but I wonder if some things aren't best kept inside. What good comes from reminiscing? When Tolly starts in about his wife and kid back home I find myself instinctively tuning out. When he asks about my home, I change the subject. I hope you don't take offense to that, Kylie. It's not that I don't miss you and love you; it's just that talking about it makes it worse. If I'm here, I'm here. When I'm home, I'm home.

Wednesday, May 22: 09:00

I didn't sleep much last night. Head's all clouded. The rain has found a steady rhythm. All this wet. Why is it that you catch colds from the rain? That's a thing I never could figure out. If it's true, I'm screwed.

Right now, Tolly's out scouting the perimeter. We received word this morning that one of the soldiers stationed NW of us spotted movement. It could be a number of things so I'm not getting excited. I've got to climb up into my perch all the same. It's been a long time since I fired a shot, but I'm not concerned. Everything has a way of clicking into place when I'm behind the scope. It's when I'm not that I have to behave like everyone else. That's the real challenge.

Wednesday, May 22: 19:25

It turned out to be nothing. Wind and water and trees playing tricks.

Thursday, May 30: 7:11 (Ha! What I wouldn't give for a Slurpie!)

Rain, rain, go away. Come again some other day. Rain, rain, go away. All the children want to play. Rain, rain, go away. Come again some other day. Rain, rain, go away. All the children want to play. Rain, rain, go away. Come again some other day. Rain, rain, go away. All the children want to play. Rain, rain, go away. Come again some other day. Rain, rain, go away. All the children want to play. Rain,

rain, go away. Come again some other day. Rain, rain, go away. All the children want to play. Rain, rain, go away. Come again some other day. Rain, rain, go away. All the children want to play. Rain, rain, go away. Come again some other day. Rain, rain, go away. All the children want to play. Rain, rain, take me away. Don't come back another day. Rain, rain, take me away. All the soldiers want to play.

Wednesday, June 5: 20:19

I'm sorry to report there hasn't been much to report. Rain still falls. Of course. What do dry socks feel like? I try to keep spirits up. Tolly spends most of his time out on patrol or else staring at weird bugs and lizards or whatever. Me, I almost stepped on a turtle yesterday. I'm better suited for seeing things that are far away. I'll try to do that with you.

Friday, June 7: 06:00

It stopped, Kylie. It stopped. Through the glistening canopy above I can see the sun!

Saturday, June 8: 19:50

While out on a solo patrol I heard movement and melted into the foliage to wait it out. Then, not ten feet in front of me, I spotted a monkey. It looked just like a monkey you'd see at the zoo. I damned near blew its head off. And it saw me, too. I know it. We looked at each other, and I swear to God the thing winked at me. Then it scurried up a tree and disappeared. When I told Tolly he made me describe it in detail. What's to really describe? It's a monkey. Apparently, Tolly's uncle is some kind of scientist employed by the government who uses primates for all kinds of experiments. Tolly used to work summers in the labs cleaning cages and learning about the different species of monkeys, etc. He wanted to know exactly where I saw the one I saw and so I told him.

I'm just happy it's something that distinguishes this day from the others.

Monday, June 10: 07:45

We heard gunfire last night. Report came back that one of the men thought he saw someone. Turns out it was a monkey. Blew it to bits. Nerves are frayed, clearly. We've been out here under poor conditions doing nothing for too long. With the rain gone and gunshots out here our cover is compromised. The Captain ordered four pairs of our platoon back to camp. Unfortunately, that didn't include us. So, now all that's left are the Captain and First Lieutenant, Tolly and me. And the monkeys. They are rhesus monkeys, a whole family of them. (Actually, a group of monkeys is called a "troop." Tolly was quick to correct me . . .) I've seen five or six of them.

Now that there are just four of us our territory has expanded. I'll need to stay focused.

Speck is distracted from reading when the bedroom door suddenly springs open. On instinct he drops the book to his chest and tries to hide it.

Nolan is filling up the space in the doorway. "I startle you?"

"No," Speck says, scooting lower under his sheets until only his head remains visible.

"See what it's like when someone barges in on you?"

"Yes."

"That's why we knock, Mr. Petro."

"I'm sorry."

Nolan softens his stance. "That book any good?"

"It's weird."

"About love?"

"War, I think."

"You think?"

"I guess it is."

Nolan scratches the back of his neck. "I've got some errands to run before work. There's food in the fridge. You be all right?"

"Sure."

"You talk to your mom?"

"I did. Last night. She won't be able to get cell phone reception for five days."

"I'll bet she's mad as hell about the bee stings and poison ivy."

Speck didn't mention these things to her mom. "Wasps. I've been learning about them online."

"Right. Keep yourself covered with calamine. I'll pick more up," he says, turning away. "Try to stay out of trouble."

II.

The drive back to Summerfield is quiet and tense. An army of clouds crowds the sky. Crowley keeps his unblinking gaze to the road. Hudson runs a finger along a reddening scratch on his arm where the old woman raked him with her fingernail.

"Menagerie, huh?" Crowley spits as they pull into the development.

"It's just a word," Hudson replies.

"No, no, it's good. I like it."

Hudson folds his hands in his lap. Crowley stops the van in front of the new house. They'll need to finish hanging drywall by the end of the week when the painters are due to arrive.

"It isn't easy," Crowley says slowly to Hudson. "I got nothing in my life but her. Because of her, too. You think she appreciates me?"

"Have you considered putting her into assisted living?"

"Can't afford it. I'm saving up." Crowley climbs out of the van and slams the door shut. Instead of walking back to the house he steps into the center of the cul-de-sac. "Maybe I'll buy one of these houses," he points and spins around in a slow circle indicating the six newly built, unoccupied structures standing tiredly in the heat. The roofs are slanted in prayer; the houses are hoping for relief from the sky.

"Maybe."

"I know you don't think I ever will," Crowley saunters over to the van. "I see the way you look down at me. You'll be gone in a few weeks, and you won't remember a thing about me or this job. I'll still be here. I might not be able to afford any of these houses, but this here is my home."

"I don't look down . . ."

Before he has a chance to react Crowley grabs Hudson by the shirt collar, hoists him out of the passenger seat, spins him around, and pins him to the side of the van. "You're not listening, boy." Crowley moves a thick arm around Hudson and leans into him.

"Get the fuck off," Hudson shouts. His face is burning against the heat of the van. The young man does not have the strength to break free.

"Easy, now," Crowley says. He presses his bulge hard into Hudson's backside. "I'll let you in on a little secret."

Hudson's heart races. He can feel his mind detaching itself from the moment. He is quick to remove himself from this position and instead occupy the point of view of someone looking on as if this is a scene in a movie. And the moment will cut away in just a few seconds.

"I put animals in the walls," Crowley says with a hard pelvic thrust before releasing the boy.

Hudson throws a wild punch, spitting and cursing and crouching in a defensive posture as he turns to face Crowley.

The man unpeels his shirt and drops it to the concrete. Tattooed on his chest and arms are fierce-looking creatures. With his arms raised high he bellows at the clouds, "Behold my menagerie!"

While Crowley indicates the different animals sketched on his body— a tiger, a wolf, a badger, a shark, a bear—and then points to the corresponding houses in which he's walled his mother's figurines, Hudson wipes spittle away from his mouth with the back of his hand and then, summoning all the power in his body, jams his bent fingers through the yellow eye of the blackbird sketched across Crowley's chest, splintering ribs. He makes a fist around the heart until it pops and oozes.

"Hey, dude, wipe that look off your face," the man says when he notices Hudson isn't paying attention to the artwork. "You like what you felt when I was up against you, huh?"

Hudson stands upright, breaking out of his fantasy.

"Thought I had a hard-on for you? You wish." Crowley reaches his hand deep into the pocket of his jeans and pulls out a glass crocodile with a happy smile and big, round, gentle eyes. He holds it aloft in his palm. "My brother got to this one before I had a chance to snatch it some Valentine's Day years ago. Like always, Mom loved it. Today's the day we put him in our house. The foyer's the best place there is. When the owners come in after a long day of work, 'Honey, I'm home!' this little guy will be waiting. It'll still be there long after the next owners come and the ones after that . . ."

"You used me as a diversion."

"Look here," Crowley says, exposing his shoulder so that Hudson can see the crocodile—teeth bared and tail poised for attack—tattooed there among the aggravated red skin. "My latest installment. I told you they do the best work at Ink Vein. Wanna touch it?"

"You'll say I stole it."

The man stops beaming and lowers his arms. He sighs through his nose and bends down to fetch his shirt. "It's complicated, Beanpole. And it's none of your business. All the animals the halfie bought her I seal into the houses. Better that I take them so she can't sit there all damned day staring and daydreaming about her dead son. That son-of-a bitch is gone. I'm sure she's sick to death right about now. Probably took her five seconds to realize it was missing. You think she would have noticed if I took one of the animals I bought for her?"

Hudson flinches when Crowley tries to pat him on the back. "No way in hell. Now let's get back to work." Taking a few steps toward the house, the man stops and says, "One of these days I'm going to strap her down to her wheelchair and give her a strip tease. Show her what I've done with Gabe's animals. Let her see how they look on *my* skin."

Hudson has to battle the urge to flee into the woods. In his head he counts backwards from twenty to calm himself. When the first droplets of rain slap against the pavement they seem so foreign.

After Hudson's father leaves Speck tucks his head back under the covers and falls asleep. Later, the urge to use the bathroom pulls him awake. When he is finished and in the hall he hears a faint scratching and whimpering issuing from beneath the front door. Who knows how long this has been going on. On the other side is the white dog, Pepper, crouched low, tongue and tail flapping.

"Hey, boy," Speck says, "come on in."

The dog doesn't hesitate. With a short bark he's inside and jumping up to play. And, just like that the day is sharper and worthwhile. They tussle roughly in the little living room. "I guess your leg has healed." The boy tries to keep his balance when Pepper leaps at his chest. "All right, let me get dressed, and we'll go for a walk. Wait here."

Instead of returning the journal to the mantle the boy slides it beneath his pillow. He re-applies the calamine and dresses in his only pair of jeans and a T-shirt. He'd rather brave the heat wearing long pants than combat the desire to scratch his legs all day.

Back in the living room Pepper is ruthlessly clawing his ear with his hind paws.

"I know how you feel," Speck says, stepping over to help. When he's close enough and running his nails through the dog's fur Speck sees how filthy the dog is. "Everyone's been paying attention to your brother and forgotten you. How would you like a bath?"

The dog continues to scratch his ear.

While the warm water is filling the tub Speck roots around for soap and a brush. The best he can find is an old toilet scrub. "Don't worry; this thing probably hasn't been used in years. It'll feel good, anyway. Hop in."

Pepper obeys. When he's in, Speck switches to shower mode and water cascades over the dog, which startles him enough to shake and spray the bathroom and the boy.

"Damn it," Speck scolds. "Don't do that." He peels his shirt off. "I just put this on. Stay here," he insists. Stepping outside, he drapes his shirt over the porch rail to dry. He doesn't notice the gathering clouds on the horizon and returns inside.

At first Speck thinks his eyes are playing tricks on him—the adjustment from outside light to inside light fiddling with hues—when he sees the stream of pinkish-colored water draining off Pepper's fur and staining the pool. The color doesn't change after the boy forces a few hard blinks. Hurrying over, Speck discovers that this is blood. And with the fur flattened the boy can make out tiny dark-colored insects clinging like irregular flaps of skin all over the dog's body.

"Oh," Speck says, recoiling, "ticks." The boy instinctively scratches his bare chest. "This is bad."

Pepper lifts his hind legs and nearly slips when he tries to get at his ear.

"It's all right, boy. Don't do that. How about you sit?" Speck unplugs the drain and lets the bloody water spiral away. He turns the water off and flinches when Pepper shakes again. Getting serious, the boy commands the dog down. When Pepper finally relaxes, Speck kneels next to the tub to investigate. He spreads the fur and, with his fingernails, tries to pluck one of the fattest ticks off. With effort, the body yanks out leaving the tiny, parasitic head imbedded. Frustrated, Speck looks around the bathroom for something to help. In the medicine cabinet he finds old balms, toothpaste, and tweezers. Glancing for a moment at his water-flecked image staring back at him the mirror, he says, "This is a start."

There's nothing helpful in the hall closet. He considers and then discards the idea of a paring knife in the kitchen. In the living room his eyes drift to the mantle. There, in the smallest, cherry-colored coffin-shaped box with engraved flowers and a pewter top are matches, he remembers. Carrying the box with both hands, Speck returns to the bathroom where Pepper's waiting nervously wagging his tail.

"I need you to stay still. This isn't going to be easy. Let's start down here." Speck parts the fur and finds a tick clinging near the base of the tail. After removing all the wooden matches Speck sets the box atop the toilet lid. He strikes the head of the match against the sandpapery flint on the matchbox and watches as the sudden pop of flame ignites—a little magic here. Pepper retracts his tail. The boy shakes the fire out with a quick flick of his wrist. Then, leaning close, he lowers the still-hot tip of the match onto the backside of the engorged tick. When the insect rears Speck snips it with the tweezers and hoists it writhing away. "Got you!" Searching for a suitable place to deposit it, Speck narrows in on the wooden box. "Can't suck on anything in there," he says, lowering it in.

When he discovers three more ticks in Pepper's hindquarters Speck snaps flame into the match, extinguishes it, and is able to tweeze all of them with a single stick. He sets them into the box. To his credit, the dog, other than whimper occasionally, behaves. He senses some good is being done. By the time the boy is up around Pepper's neck there are two dozen hapless blood-bloated parasites rolling around the bottom of the box. The gooseflesh on Speck's arms has subsided now that he has made progress. He is no longer repulsed by the insects, just determined to exterminate them. When he eases back Pepper's ear to continue, however, the boy's arm hairs spike again. Clustered together like a spoonful of raisins are more ticks than anywhere else on the dog's body. Despite his best efforts Speck has to step away and rake his nails up and down his arms and chest before returning to work. His determination overcomes disgust.

"They must like your neck," he says, patting Pepper's head softly. He strikes a match, waves it out, applies the heat, plucks four ticks, and drops them in the box. When he returns his attention to his work, Speck notices movement around the dog's inner earflap. This catches him off guard. The blood-sated ticks don't move much. With a deft plunge, Speck snags the insect before it can sneak deeper down into the dog's ear canal. He lifts it into the air to inspect it. Unlike the floundering ticks with the expanding bodies, this thing is compact—missile-shaped—more like a beetle than a spider. It is dun-colored with a crimson luster. As he turns it over Speck can see a patch of tiny eggs—like the finest cottage cheese—tucked beneath paddle-like wings. The multi-refracted eyes stare blankly at Speck from a slick, antennaed head.

"What the hell are you?" Speck says. He drops it among the ticks, re-places several matches, and then seals the lid on top of the box. "That thing will crawl out if it can. We'll toss the rest in the toilet."

When he's finished, Speck lathers Pepper with soap and washes him again. He turns the shower on and watches until the blood in the water disappears. Afterwards, he towels the dog off. "When your brother gets better, I'll take care of him, too. If he lets me."

Pepper, spent, trots to the front door. Speck opens it and finds a curtain of rain cascading in sheets across the porch roof. The dog hesitates. Then he taps toward the steps leading to Gus's apartment and curls into a tight white ball. Speck scowls at his drenched T-shirt plastered to the rail and then returns inside. Whatever joy he felt earlier has evaporated.

The boy sets the cherry-colored coffin-shaped box back on the mantle. He shakes it a few times to hear the insects and matches rattle. He wonders how long it will sit there unopened and what the person will think when he or she discovers what's inside. Here is a little mystery the boy has created, a secret for some faraway stranger to puzzle through. Speck will always remember the sacrifice these parasites have made, insignificant as it may seem. He won't forget the suffocating death in the box on the mantle, in his head. The blood upon his hands.

12.

Wasps are well represented as mascots in the world of sports. The NBA has the New Orleans Hornets, the NCAA celebrates the Georgia Tech Yellow Jackets, the Minnesota Swarm play lacrosse, and the London Wasps are a feisty rugby team. In some cases, the mascot is fuzzy, warm, and spirited with a wide smile. Spectators enjoy the comical way the insect meanders along the sideline— working with the cheer squad—or when it bounds up the stadium stairs pausing long enough to collect children into exaggerated wings for snapshots from eager parents. Other promoters choose to focus on the toughness of the species; stingers become razor-sharp swashbuckling swords and eyes are slanted in a fierce, soul-piercing stare. No matter how the mascot is depicted, when the home team is winning the audible buzz emanating from the excited crowd often helps inspire the team to victory.

Crowley pulls the van into the Muller parking lot near the front house, in a downpour. After walling the crocodile into the foyer, Hudson and the man spent the rest of the afternoon cleaning downstairs so that they can start fresh upstairs first thing in the morning.

"I'm letting you out here," Crowley says, unwilling to drive down the muddy road to the pink house.

"That's fine," Hudson replies.

"I'm not taking any chances getting stuck. You'll have to get wet."

"Fine." Hudson slides out. He hunches his shoulders and begins to walk down the slick slope of road. Before he is far along he hears the van's horn beep. Turning, he sees Madison standing on the porch with her arms folded glaring at Crowley who is shouting something through the window. Hudson is surprised he hadn't seen her.

Without thinking about it, Hudson bends down and finds a fist-sized rock, straightens, and pitches it at the van. It shatters a taillight. Hudson blinks a few times questioning whether or not he just did when he thinks he did.

What happens next happens quickly. Crowley flies out of the van and attacks. He punches Hudson in the face, and when the young man covers his mouth, he punches him in the ribs, and when he crouches low to cover his midsection, the man drives his elbow down hard at the base of Hudson's neck sending him flat into the mud. By the time Crowley begins to kick Hudson, Madison has sprinted out into the rain brandishing a thin knife she uses to cut away bottle wrappings. She threatens to stab.

Crowley steps back. He puts his hands up defensively. "Hold it there, Sunshine," he says. "I'm done with your fairy."

"I will slit your throat."

"Oh, I doubt that. Your family prefers to slice wrists, right?"

Madison grinds her teeth. She fights to maintain her composure. "If you don't go," she says evenly, "I'm calling the cops."

"Shit," Crowley slurs as he turns and trudges back to the van. "You need a good muzzle, bitch. And you better keep your boyfriend on a short leash or I'll put him down."

Madison turns her attention to Hudson who is prone on the ground. "Hey," she whispers, shaking him, "let's get you cleaned up."

Hudson struggles to breathe. His mouth is choked with mud, he thinks, but then, rising and spitting, he sees it is his blood washing down his shirtfront. With his head spinning and through a fog he sees Crowley blow a kiss before climbing into his van and fishtailing away. The tires send a spray of sludge over the two.

With effort, Madison directs Hudson into the house, up the stairs, and into her bathroom. He slumps on the toilet seat while she turns on the faucet in the bathtub.

"That bastard," she says, dumping liquid soap into the steaming water.

Hudson works a loose tooth out and spits a rope of blood into the sink. "Glad I had braces," Hudson says, trying to lighten the mood. As badly as he feels, he can't repress the thrill. So often he merely fantasizes about acting and is left feeling cowardly in the aftermath. While things didn't turn out the way he would have liked just *doing something* is something.

Madison helps Hudson out of his clothes and into the too-hot bath water that quickly clouds copper with mud and blood. To his surprise, he feels no shame reclining naked in the tub. She has, after all, just seen him beaten down. What's there to lose now?

"Why did you throw that rock?" Madison asks. She withdraws a washcloth from a drawer and uses it to scrub away mud at her elbow.

"Why don't you join me?"

A quick blush flushes Madison's cheeks as she considers. "My mom could be home any minute."

"We'll hear her."

"The water is filthy."

Hudson reaches around his back to unplug the drain. While the dirty water washes down he twists the knobs to refill it with clean water. "I'll close my eyes until you're ready."

Madison grins. "All right," she says softly, moving to lock the bathroom door. "Don't peek."

"I'm really starting to feel better," Hudson says as he splashes around.

"I bet." She takes her clothes off, removes her bracelets, and sets everything neatly atop the counter. Then she slides into the tub with her back to Hudson. She reclines into his chest and lets the soapy water consume her. Hudson suppresses the pain he feels in his bruised body as she leans against him. There is no amount of hurt that could pull him away from this moment. He cups water and pours it over her head, careful not to get any in her eyes, and then he massages her neck.

"That's nice," Madison says, relaxing.

"Is it all right if that gets wet?" Hudson runs his fingers along Madison's arm to the bandage at her wrist.

"Yes. But it's probably time to take it off. It makes me sick that Crowley is the only person that knows what it is," she says, turning to face Hudson. She extends her arm and says, "You do it."

"Yeah?"

"I'm ready."

"All right," Hudson says. "You like it quick or slow?"

"We're talking about band aids, right?" Madison raises her eyebrow.

While she's distracted, Hudson yanks it off and sets it on side of the tub. There, tattooed on her wrist, is a tiny blonde-haired female with curled horns atop her head. She has blue wings and is wearing a red coat, long black gloves, yellow pants, red boots, and goggles. The creature is straddling a large bomb and appears to be descending with a look of fierce determination. "Cool," Hudson manages to say through his busted lips. "What does it mean?"

"That's Fifi," Madison says. She pulls her arm back and folds it across her chest. "Fifinella, technically. She's the mascot for the Women Air Force Service Pilots. My grandmother used to be a WASP." She studies Hudson's face. "She used to call me her little Gremlin."

"It's cute."

Madison repositions herself in Hudson's arms. "The WASPs got Fifi from a book called, *The Gremlins*. My grandmother read it to me all the time. You know it?"

"I saw the movie."

"They're not the same. In the fairy tale, there are these little creatures that help the British Air Force fight the Nazis. The gremlins would tinker with the airplane engines and then parachute to safety while the bad guys crashed. Boom!" Madison says, splashing water in Hudson's face.

"Yeah, that's not like the movie at all." Hudson takes the opportunity to press his mouth against hers. When they pull away he says, "Thank you."

"What for?"

"Defending me. Cleaning me off. Watching out for my brother. Letting me see your tattoo. Showing me your bedroom . . ."

"Ha," Madison says, stepping out of the water and grabbing a towel. "Aren't you presumptuous?"

Hudson splashes out behind her. He tugs playfully at her towel. "Give me that. I'm cold."

"What about my mom?" Madison says, unlocking the bathroom door and leading him into her bedroom."

"I guess we'll have to make this quick," Hudson says with a smile.

Plugging his headphones into his ears, Speck takes the journal out to the den and plops down on the chair to read. He cranks up Bach's concerto and picks up where he left off:

Wednesday, June 12: 15:00

Just a quick note today. While I was out in unfamiliar terrain I came upon a cave. I almost walked right by. It was well camouflaged with vines and bushes. Back in the desert they trained us to look for hideouts in the mountains. Fissures can turn into labyrinths. The protocol for investigation is to first scour the ground for landmines and then cautiously creep up next to the mouth. Then you're supposed to look for tracks and any sign of movement. I couldn't see or hear anything. It didn't occur to me at the time, but that was kind of odd, too. No birds or bugs. I guess it's possible that there are still places in the world where people have never been. That's how it felt to me, any-way—like a discovery.

The next thing you're supposed to do is use an extending rod which has a mirror affixed to it. It's supposed to prevent you from getting your head blown off. So I used mine. Not that I expected to see anyone. Inside was just dark. I got out my pocket flashlight and shimmied in. When I was about five feet deep I heard this unusual buzzing. It's hard to describe, is what I mean. Sounded more like ringing in your ears— you know, like when someone is thinking about you—rather than like all the damned mosquitoes I've been hearing. When I panned the light across the top of the cave in front of me I caught my breath. There were wasps. Hundreds of them clustered around dozens of nests all over the place. Made my skin crawl. You know how I mentioned that the brand of mosquitoes over here are bigger than New York mosquitoes? The same thing can be said about these wasps. And, they weren't black and yellow; they were black and crimson, maybe? It was hard to tell. They looked like they could do some serious damage if provoked. All I know is that I'm grateful for my sniper training because I held my breath and steadied my heart and backed the hell out of there.

When I told Tolly about them, he got all excited. I guess he's into bugs, too. I gave him directions to the cave but suggested that he leave it alone. Maybe some places aren't meant to be found?

Saturday, June 15: 18:50

Since the rain has stopped the mosquitoes have relented a bit. Ei-ther that or I've just grown used to them. Or, my skin has adapted. Or, I've got no more blood left. Or, I'm turning into one. Buzz, buzz.

Not much is going on. Nobody has seen any signs of anybody. This part of the planet has been forgotten. I'm beginning to question our intelligence. I can't imagine we'll be here much longer. That's not up to me to decide.

On a different note, Tolly has been scheming. He's an industrious son-of-a bitch. He's concocted a plan to get us out of here. I don't just mean out of the jungle, I mean out of the country and back home. His idea? Catch monkeys. That's right. I know it sounds ridiculous. It reads stupid when I write it down like this. The way he explains it—with a lot of energy—makes some sense, though. As I might have mentioned, the monkeys that we've spotted are called rhesus macaws. Apparently, these are the species that we use for animal testing. Tolly says that labs prefer to use wild primates rather than ones that they breed in captivity. Don't ask me why. I just know that Tolly's sure that he can convince the higher-ups to let us escort one or two back to the States. Tolly says there's a lab right in New York City and, if he can contact his uncle, somehow, he can verify that this is important . . . I don't know. Sounds convoluted to me. Monkey business! Sheesh.

Anyway, what else better do I have to do?

Sunday, June 16: 14:00

We've spoken to Captain and gotten encouraging news. We're pulling out of this place on Friday unless we hear or see anything suspicious. And that's not all. We were told that our tour will be over in the next six months. Home by Christmas.

But, there's more. Crazy Tolly kept pressing the monkey issue, and they looked into it. Just like that. So happens Tolly is right. They talked with his uncle. We do get monkeys from nearby, but rarely here in Nuristan. After all, this place is not particularly safe. What I'm getting at is this: there's a Navy cargo ship docked in the Persian Gulf leaving for New York at the end of the month. If we happen to snag a monkey we'll secure a ticket on board as escorts! We have until Friday. It's a long shot, Kylie, and I don't want to get my hopes up. Still, I'll do whatever I can.

Sunday, June 16: 22:30

After returning from our rounds Tolly and I talked awhile. He told me that he isn't all that surprised about the government's interest in fresh monkeys. I guess his uncle is pretty high up in rank. Tolly has all kinds of stories which he's witnessed or else heard from his uncle. It's all classified. What he could tell me I wouldn't want to share with you anyway. It ain't pretty.

What I'm getting at is that I think I'd feel a little guilty if we did manage to catch one of the critters. The testing doesn't bother Tolly one bit. Better a monkey than a human. I get that, of course. And I'd damned near do anything to get back home. Maybe, if we do get lucky, he will be used for breeding. That wouldn't be half bad!

Moving on to a different topic—how to catch a monkey. I can't possibly imagine we'll be successful at this. The closest I've ever been to one was that first time by accident. (The one that winked at me.) Tolly says that we start by observing their habits, their patterns, their routines. We need to hone in on one particular troop. He says, like people, they tend to do things in repetition. He has already identified a group which lives about a quarter mile from our tree house. He's been taking notes. A regular Jane Goodall! He knows which are the fastest, strongest, and the weakest. The adult animals we'd never be able to handle (they are stronger than any human). The old timers hang out in the treetops and avoid the ground. Our best bet, then, is an adolescent. As far as he can tell there are four that fit the bill.

Speck is pulled out of his journal not so much because he hears the sound as much as he senses it. He sits upright, tugging the earplugs out, and stays still, listening. For a moment there is nothing but the hypnotic rain clamor. Then, very softly, he hears the unmistakable sound of scratching. Something is clawing away at the floorboards beneath his feet. Instinctively, Speck tucks his legs up onto the couch.

The sound is, as best as the boy can tell, coming from beneath the center of the room. He waits until the fear begins to abate, and he can reason this through. Something is underneath the house, but it is not, as his imagination wants to lead him, a person. A zombie. If that were the case he'd hear low moaning. What he occasionally hears, punctuating the scratching, is a kind of high-pitched trill. It is a mouse or a rat, then. Though it seems more powerful than even the big rats he's seen patrolling the subways back home. The rug faintly vibrates. Perhaps it is one of the dogs.

This possibility gets the boy off the couch. He hurries to the center of the room and throws back the rug and is caught off guard by what's there. Etched into the flooring is a small door, a hatch, some kind of secret passage. A handle has been carved into the wood and a lock secures a deadbolt.

"Sultan?" Speck whispers forcefully, dropping to his knees. "Pepper?"

The feverish clawing stops. Speck tries to control his breathing. In the crack between the panel and the floor there is a wink of light reflected off the animal's eye that the boy sees peering back at him all reddish-brown and wild. And then the animal manages to stick a bloodied claw through and, emitting a howl, lunge hard enough against the hatch to send the boy onto his back. The hinges hold, and the lock rattles. The animal attacks again.

Glancing around the room, Speck tries to find something to put on top of the door to keep it held down. With effort, he slides the couch away from the wall and over the secret panel. Then the boy backs into the family room holding the journal to his chest. The animal crashes against the door again, growling now, then abruptly quiets and stops. Speck waits in the aftermath for some clarity to take hold. A clock in the kitchen on the stove he never noticed is ticking away. With all of his attention on the floor, the boy leaps into the air when he hears a loud thud from above in Gus's apartment.

Outside, the gray is giving way to dark. The rain continues to fall, dampening the gloomy landscape. Speck worries about his brother. He should be here by now. All at once the boy feels an irrepressible wave of sadness. He has never been this alone before. He pinches his eyes closed and battles back his emotions.

After a while, Speck opens his eyes, better. He'll work through all this. Creeping up the steps, the boy stands in the dark and knocks tentatively on Gus's door. He has not seen or heard from the old man all day. After several unanswered moments have passed, he presses his face to the wood and calls out. Finally, the door partially opens.

From what Speck can tell in the small, semi-illuminated space, Gus looks like a different man. His hair is frazzled, and the whiskers along the side of his face are caked with what looks like dried blood. His eyes are milky, and they are having trouble focusing on the boy. When Gus turns his head Speck sees that a battered Q-tip has been jammed deep into the old man's ear.

"Are you all right?" Speck asks.

Gus draws his arm out from behind the door and runs the backside of his hand across his chin. Clutched in his fist is a gun.

"I heard a noise," the boy says, keeping his eyes on the pistol.

"What?" Gus asks, returning his hand out of sight behind the door.

"Your ear."

"I got a tickle."

"I think there's an animal under the house."

"My dog is not well." Gus swallows hard and shakes his head vigorously. "You know what you do when an animal's not well, don't you?"

Speck takes a step backwards down the stairs.

"Same thing you do when a man—or woman—isn't well."

"Maybe I should call a doctor."

"There's been a storm crowding up my head for a long time," he says slowly. "Tonight, I feel it dissipating. Maybe it's the wine. Might have finally gotten it right."

When Gus speaks Speck can see his teeth are stained red.

"Now, if you'll excuse me, I've got to get back to my sick dog and this exquisite elixir." Gus loses his balance as he slams the door shut. The boy hears the old man stumble to the floor, laughing. "Mercy," he calls out. "Mercy me."

13.

Just after Hudson lightly kisses Madison the headlights from Clara's car bending into the long driveway paint stripes across his chest. He holds a meek hand into the drizzle to let her know that he sees her, and he keeps his head tucked close to his shoulder so that she cannot get a clear look at his battered face.

In the short distance from the new house to the pink house Hudson never puts a foot on the ground. He feels so clean beneath the filthy clothes. In the space between houses he's not thinking about the repercussions of his actions today or tonight. Nor does he pay any attention to the nagging guilt that he feels for abandoning his brother all day or not making any effort to spend time with his father. As he skims along he tastes the flavor of the rain mingling with the perfume upon his skin. He's letting the imprint of the moment sink in.

In the house Speck is sitting at the kitchen counter with his back to the door, headphones in. He doesn't turn when Hudson enters.

"Hey," Hudson says, surveying the house. "You've done some redecorating?"

The boy takes a bite of food and says, "There's macaroni on the stove if you're hungry."

"Thanks," Hudson says. He cautiously eases into the kitchen to find a plate and figure out the angle his brother's playing. "How are you doing?"

"You look like shit," Speck says.

Hudson uses a wooden spatula to scrape the last of the cold food from the pot onto his plate. He begins to eat. It is painful to chew. He waits a few moments to give his brother time to let go of whatever anger he's got pent up.

Speck scratches his leg and then takes a gulp of milk. He narrows his eyes and scowls at his older brother. "We should call a doctor."

"I won't talk to you with those in your ears."

Speck makes an exaggerated show of tugging the earplugs out. "Tada," he says, slapping them onto the counter. "That better? You have my undivided attention."

Hudson runs his tongue over the space where his incisor used to be. It stings and makes the macaroni and cheese taste like copper. He pushes the plate away. "I am here, Speck," he says.

"About time."

"I know it."

"It's been a fucked up day."

"Go ahead and keep swearing if it makes you feel better."

"Thanks, mom."

"You talk to her today?" Hudson steps around the counter to inspect his brother's irritated skin.

"I did. I told her everything is wonderful."

"Come with me into the bathroom."

"That pink shit doesn't work, and I'm tired of looking like a fool wearing it."

"It does make you look silly. You blend in with the house."

"Don't placate me."

"Fine," Hudson says. He hobbles into the den and, with a groan, begins to shove the couch back against the wall. Speck watches him, keeping quiet.

The animal beneath the house has been resting, and it hurls itself against the hatch with renewed energy.

"What the hell is that?" Hudson says, peering over the arm of the couch.

"It's not a zombie," Speck says.

Hudson repositions the couch how Speck had it. "You might have mentioned this."

"You wouldn't have believed me."

"Does my dad know?"

"He's a ghost."

Hudson walks back into the kitchen. He rummages through drawers until he finds a flimsy flashlight that casts a feeble light. "Come on," he says to his brother and makes his way outside without waiting for a reply.

Speck willingly follows. He has to nearly run to catch up to his brother's rapid loping strides. After a short distance, almost to the grapevines, Hudson stops next to an opening in the earth. "We forgot to put the cover back," he says.

Speck peers into the black. "What is it?"

"A bomb shelter." Hudson eases to his knees and plays the light down past the rungs of the hook ladder to the concrete bottom eight feet down.

"That makes sense, knowing Gus. He thinks the sky is falling."

Hudson shines the flashlight in his brother's eyes. "How much time have you been spending . . ."

From below there is a scampering and a low growl. Hudson trains the light back down. There, in the faint glow, is an enormous raccoon—the size of a Chow—with teeth bared. One of the creature's ears has been sliced to ribbons while the other is scratched away to a bloody nub. Its eyes take the light and spit it back red.

"It must have fallen in," Hudson says. "Probably rabid."

"Do you think it can climb back out?"

"I don't know. I wish we could put it out of its misery."

"Gus has a gun," Speck says.

"What are you talking about?" Hudson turns his attention to his brother.

"The old man has a pistol. From when he was in the war, I guess."

"He showed it to you?"

"Not exactly. I just saw it. I think he's going to kill Sultan."

Hudson frowns. The elation he felt fifteen minutes ago feels like a distant memory. "Help me slide the cover back on," he says, rising.

The two maneuver the lid into place over the hole.

"We're just going to leave him down there?" Speck asks as they head back hunched under the persistent rain.

Hudson can no longer beat back the exhaustion he feels. He ignores his younger brother until they are back inside the house. "Two things," he says. "Stay away from the old man and forget about the raccoon."

Speck opens his mouth to protest but thinks better of it. He's much more comfortable letting his brother take charge. "What raccoon?"

"Good. I need to sleep. You coming?"

"I'm actually going to read a while first."

"World's upside down."

"You going to tell me about your face?"

"I pissed off my boss."

"Still have a job?"

"No. But I might have a girlfriend."

"Really?"

"Enough questions, kid. Listen, I'm sorry for all this. I know it's lousy here. I'll do better."

"Not your responsibility. It's not fun around here, but at least it's not boring. Plus, this journal that I found is really interesting. It's about this soldier who discovers these badass wasps, just like the ones in the woods, and . . ."

"Great, great," Hudson says. He winces as he removes his shirt and then enters the bedroom. "Don't say up too late. We'll talk more in the morning."

After his brother is gone Speck throws himself on the chair with his back to the den. He puts his headphones on and cranks the classical music. He picks up where he left off:

Monday, June 17: 19:00

All last night Tolly built a cage using cedar wood and twine. It needs to be extra-strong because monkeys are tough to keep locked, apparently. The cage is not very big, and it's tied with a rope handle on top so you can carry it like a suitcase and move around the terrain without much difficulty.

Since this morning he has been working on traps. I've had to pick up his scouting territory so he can work. That doesn't bother me any. The sun has been out these last few days and, although it's hot, it's bearable in the shade.

Tolly's got three kinds of traps. One is a box trap. The idea is for a monkey to walk into a small wood-slatted box for some fruit and trip a latch which will drop a door down behind it. The second trap is made out of netting Tolly stripped from our tent lining. You're supposed to hide the net under leaves on the forest floor. It has been stretched tight with a rope snaking up to a tree branch so that when a monkey steps on it, the net closes over, and the rope hoists the thing up off the ground. The third trap is something Tolly put up in a tree he thinks the monkeys might visit. It's just one of the camouflage sacks we use to hold our sleeping bags stretched between two branches. He smeared monkey crap all over it, for some reason, and when the creature crawls in, the weight of the thing will push through the branches, and the rope at the top of the sack will tighten over it. Unlike me, he's optimistic.

I don't think any of these things will work. This forest is filled with booby traps and mines and all kinds of nasty things and you just don't hear explosions and see charred monkey meat all around. They've adapted. Our best bet is to snipe one in the shoulder or something, haul it in, and hope it heals by the time we get back to the States. Should I get the chance I just might do this. It's been forever since I fired my weapon.

Wednesday, June 19: 07:22

The rain returned last night with a vengeance. Since our lean-to has been compromised in order to make Tolly's dubious nets, getting through to morning was not pleasant. Now that it's morning, it still sucks. Everything in the forest is hunkering down. With so many recent dry days the packed dirt is going to turn into runny mud, and I can already smell the stench of it. I just have to hold on for two more days. With or without a monkey, I'm eager to get out of this place.

I've got to go now. I hear Tolly beckoning. I don't think he's content to stay huddled here. He'll want to check on those traps.

Wednesday, June 19: 20:18

The monkeys are nowhere to be found. Tolly can't explain it. The rain has stopped—it was just a storm not a monsoon. Tomorrow we'll redouble our efforts.

Thursday, June 20: 22:45

Hell, Kylie, I got one! I know it's hard to believe. And no, I didn't shoot it. (If I did, I'd have to toss this journal. There's no way that kind of detail would pass through the screening.) Here's what happened: This morning was fine weather. Not as humid as it's been and nice. Easy-to-breathe-in weather. So, as usual, Tolly went out to check his traps, and I first walked his perimeter and then started along my own. It was noon around this time and most of the mud had dried. Felt like a hike. Birds and bugs and frogs and things were chirping like usual, and then, quite suddenly, the sound stopped. I don't know how long I walked in that silence before I took notice of it. And, sure enough, I was by that old cave again. I could see it hiding ahead of me. Only this time, there were wasps buzzing around the entrance. As I said before, these aren't your blue-blooded American wasps; these things look like they flew right out of hell. They make my skin crawl. Anyway, I froze and was about to turn back when I caught movement in the brush not too far from the cave. And there he was. A young rhesus monkey bobbing around like he'd just gone eight rounds with a gorilla! The little guy was clearly stunned. A cloud of wasps was hanging over him. As you know, I don't consider myself to be the bravest soldier in the world, but there was no way I was going to let a bunch of insects get in the way of home. So I sprinted over to that monkey, scooped him up in my arms like a football, and kept on running through the trees and away from the cave. Most of the wasps flew away. One of them stung me, I realize now, but at the time, I didn't even feel it. And that little guy hardly even struggled as I rushed back to camp. Tolly was astonished. Couldn't believe it. We situated our new friend in the cage and just sort of stared at each other dumbfounded until dusk came on.

All evening we've been excitedly talking. We're not going to say anything to Captain. We'll just march on back with it, not make a big deal, and let him honor his word.

Tolly told me the first thing he was going to do when we get back home is buy me the most expensive drink they've got in the most expensive bar in the city. He's acting like I'm some kind of hero!

The truth is that the little guy is hurt. He's been badly stung. Since I've had time for my adrenaline rush to fade I can understand a fraction of what he must be going through. Where that wasp stung me in the neck there's a welt the size of a walnut that's throbbing. I dressed it up with peroxide, and it still stings. Plus it made me a bit loopy. Those bastards must carry some kind of heavy dose of poison in their stings because I can sure feel it. The monkey's got welts all up and down his body. I pity him. Tolly has been tending to it, and he seems to know what he's doing. He told me it just needs to survive until we are on the ship. Tolly's determined to keep it alive, even if he has to perform mouth-to-mouth, so he can get back to his family.

Me, well, I realize how insensitive this all sounds. I know. But I'm telling you if I didn't show up when I did I'm pretty sure those wasps would have gone right on stinging him. Surely, he'd be dead. Now who can say what his fate will be? All I know is that he has altered mine.

I better turn in. It's getting late. We've got a long trek back tomorrow. It's hard to believe my time here is nearly done. Am I grateful. I don't know what I'm looking forward to doing most. I think what I'd like to do is just walk around town or through the mall and just be with people like me. I'd like to sit on a bench with some ice cream (mint chocolate chip) and blend into the crowd.

Sunday, June 23: 19:00

The sky is clear, and I am aboard the USS Springfield ready to set sail for New York City, New York! We will leave under the cover of night and, if all goes well, we'll arrive in the United States in six or seven days. My time here is done (unless they call me back for a third tour, of course . . .). And while this isn't a pleasure cruise across the Atlantic (in fact, they've got me working the latrines first thing in the morning and doing dishes for lunch and dinner), my days of being a sniper are behind me. I never had to take a life. When I handed over my rifle I felt an enormous weight lift. I don't envy the next fool who has to heft it around, that's for sure.

When we got back to our camp in Nuristan after a long hike in sporadic rain Tolly and I gathered what things we had and, with our monkey friend, we climbed aboard an old jeep that had been around a while and could be spared, and started the difficult drive to the Persian Gulf. That wasn't easy. Forget about the terrain, which is treacherous to say the least, there are military units all up and down the weather-beaten roadways, and it seems like we stopped every other hour to identify who we were and what we were doing. Our answer, transporting a monkey, wasn't easy to explain.

For the most part the monkey has behaved indifferently. It drools and is reluctant to eat. Tolly has coaxed it into drinking water and fruit juice, and it's in stable condition, as far as I can tell. Oh, and we've named it. Got tired of called it "the monkey" or "little guy" or whatever. Tolly wanted to call it Gent Jr., after me, obviously. I said no way. He suggested Billy or Little William. Also dumb. He refused to call it anything that didn't somehow reference me. Anyway, we finally settled on "Willy." Of course, nobody has ever called me "Willy" before (it's a terrible nickname). I can live with it because it reminds me of Willy Wonka and the Chocolate Factory. I don't remember the story exactly, but I do remember a golden ticket. That's Willy, for sure.

Tolly and I have been given our own cubby, which has two cots, a closet, and a chair. Plus, a porthole. We put caged Willy atop the chair and opened the window so he could get some fresh air. He ate a few grapes for dinner. Right now Tolly's out on deck with some of the sailors. He's eager to meet people. I don't blame him. Me, I prefer to just keep to myself and rest. I'll babysit Willy.

My hope is to catch a train from New York and be in Rochester in time for the Fourth. I'll grill you up the fattest burger in town. It's funny, but I don't think I've ever missed you more than I do right now.

Speck rubs his eyes, removes the earplugs, and closes the book. He wonders when the journal was written. The entries do not reference the year. Was the soldier talking about the Independence Day that just passed? If so, maybe he and Hudson were on the same train. The soldier—Bill or William Gent—could be out in the woods looking for the journal right now. It's too hard to tell. The only way to find out is to finish reading. For now, he returns it to the chest on the mantle.

The raccoon hasn't made a peep. The house is quiet.

In the bedroom Hudson is sleeping deeply. The bruise around his mouth is purple in the limp glow of the illuminated clock numbers. It is late. Nolan should be home soon. The boy hopes to be asleep before then. Speck will likely never know what happened to his brother. He hopes Hudson landed at least one meaningful blow.

The boy slides beneath the covers and rolls to his side. He tucks the pillow between his knees and rests his head on his outstretched arm. He remembers that he hasn't had the urge to scratch his legs. The rash is either getting better or becoming familiar.

When he is nearly under Speck hears a pop, like a punctured balloon, from the upstairs, he thinks. It could be in the woods or up the road. It could be in the sky. It should be loud enough to wake Hudson, but it does not. Speck's sure the sound breaking the silence would have awoken him if he had been the one sleeping. The boy wishes that he had been asleep, that he didn't hear the sound and didn't suspect that something terrible just happened up in Gus's apartment, that maybe this was just the sound of a late-night hooligan setting off a black cat firecracker he discovered he had forgotten to explode on the Fourth. Or it was Nolan's pickup backfiring as the tired man returns home clutching a bottle of calamine cinched in a nice, clean, brown, paper bag. The front door will open any second now.

Or, maybe the old man put the dog down. Sad as that is, it's something Speck can live with. Sultan shouldn't suffer.

Fumbling around the nightstand for his radio, Speck inserts his earplugs and cranks the classical music. He wonders if he would have heard the shot—or whatever it was—over the sound of the music. He knows the name of the song that is playing; it's Beethoven's "Moonlight" sonata. He knows what's coming up next. He pinches his eyes shut and tentatively hums along.

14.

Nolan says, "I'll handle it," into the phone on his nightstand before he hangs up. His head still shrouded in fog from the road, he rises out of bed and squints at the clock. It is only eight. He has been asleep for three hours at most.

Trailing his rising anger, Nolan crashes into the boys' room.

"Son," he shouts, "get up."

Hudson is startled. The contours of a dream he can't place evaporate. His little brother, still wearing headphones, is sitting up in bed. Wiping a hand across his fat lip, Hudson tries to process the situation.

"Got a phone call from your boss just now. Care to explain?"

"No, not really." Hudson has trouble getting words around his swollen mouth.

"That job came on my word."

"That's not something I'd brag about."

"It might not mean anything to you, but it should. You busted a taillight?"

Intent on leaving before he says something he'll regret, Hudson slides out of bed and into a pair of jeans heaped on the floor. "He knocked out a tooth."

"Maybe you deserved it," Nolan blurts.

The young man lets the heat from that comment burn before hurrying into his shoes.

Speck keeps quiet on the bed.

Realizing that what he said might not have come out right Nolan takes a stab at the point he was trying to make: "You need to understand that there are consequences for our actions," he states evenly.

"Got it," Hudson replies, pushing past his father and rapidly walking down the hall. As he exits the house he slams the front door, and the windows rattle.

"Oh no you don't," Nolan hisses, striding after his son.

Speck would prefer to pull the sheets over his head, but he is on puppet strings and the marionette won't let him avoid what follows. So, he's up, earplugs still in, legs raw from an unconscious raking during the night, bare feet lifting and falling, stringing him down the hall to watch the scene unfold through the open door.

A few paces from the porch Nolan catches Hudson by the elbow and says, through clenched teeth, "This is not your house . . ."

Hudson, on strings of his own, swings his free hand around to smack Nolan across the face. The young man shakes his father off and shouts, his voice cracking—it is painful for Speck to hear—"Get off me!" Then, before hurrying along the semi-soft muddy road toward the woods, Hudson cries, "You're even worse than mom said you'd be!"

Nolan, caught off-guard, steps back and lets Hudson scamper away. The sun in the field illuminates the evaporating dew upon the shimmering grapes. A crow crests on the eave of the hangar. It offers a few brittle caws as moments pass. Eventually, Nolan turns and considers Speck. "He'll wake the old man."

"Maybe," the boy replies.

Nolan sighs. He touches the spot on his cheek where he was slapped. "You hungry?"

Speck is thrown by the question. "I think so."

"Put something on. I'm taking you to breakfast."

Hudson doesn't look back. He doesn't know where he's going. He passes the rusting machine husks, reaches the end of the dirt road, ignores the brief pursuit Pepper gives, and stomps through the low-level underbrush like he did on day one. The loose roots below trip him up, and he hacks away with his legs and arms and twists through a thicket of dense foliage before he is confronted with the small, gravelly rise and the train tracks. He doesn't think about direction as he steps from plank to plank; anywhere is better than here.

He steps right over the abandoned wasp's burrow. He passes the spot where he broke from the woods carrying Sultan. Although it'd be a long way down to the sheepish creek-outlet below, he does not hesitate short-stepping across the bridge. He doesn't take in the breathtaking view of the kidney-shaped lake carving out the gorges, like so many passengers do here through a break in the trees.

What Hudson does is keep his head down and count railroad ties. He steps on every other board, and this makes his movement quick. He stretches his sore legs. Soon the sun burns the tender skin on his neck between hair and shirt. Even as his lips dry Hudson mouths the numbers, . . . *six hundred and fifty-five, fifty-six, fifty-seven, fifty-eight* . . . He tries to hold onto the rhythm of the numbers instead of what's in his head. Forget about the morning. Forget about the image of himself as someone might see him from afar—another nobody heading nowhere with no plan. He wants everything . . . *something, anything* . . . to be *more,* and when he thinks about how he wants it to be more it is rendered so much less. So he keeps on, fighting his slippery thoughts every step of the way.

When Hudson notices the rail vibrations, at five thousand, two hundred and thirty-one ties, he hops off the tracks and into the scruff, folds his arms, licks his purple mouth, runs a hand through his sweat-drenched hair, keeps his eyes steady on the next plank where he'll continue in just a minute, and does not look at the loud train as it passes or imagine what it is that the passengers are imagining as they catch a momentary glimpse of a damaged young man standing hollow-eyed so close to danger.

"Go away!" he snaps impatiently. Then the caboose comes, and the horizon barrier lifts. In the diminishing train-rattle Hudson accidently takes stock of his situation. He is not ready to do this. He wants just numbers and the methodical footfall along the tracks. He does not want to recognize where he is. No more than eighty railroad ties ahead is the *Lakeview* trailer home development. He does not want to slowly creep up to Crowley's trailer, double-check to make sure that the van is not in the carport, or slink beneath the back window. Overhead the clouds cover the sun. A sprinkler spits staccato across someone's dead lawn, two trailers down. Rising cautiously, Hudson cups his hands and rests them lightly against the bars covering over the window into which he doesn't want to peek.

Ms. Crowley is sitting on the couch against the back wall, beneath the window. Hudson can only see her legs and knees exposed around a hiked-up nightgown. She is doing something with her hands in her lap that Hudson can't see, and she's humming—a tune that sounds familiar. After a few moments the old woman leans forward and extends her arms out to the coffee table, and things clarify for the young man; several animals from the menagerie are lined up there and she is polishing them with a thin, white terrycloth. She's just finished a porcelain rabbit that she places beside a glass turtle.

Bugs Bunny, the tune sinks in, Hudson recalls; *that's the* Looney Tunes *theme song.*

While still leaning forward Ms. Crowley fetches a bumblebee from a gathering of still-unpolished animals. Then clouds pass. Sunlight contorts around Hudson and pitches his distorted shadow into the room, and it spills across the coffee table. Ms. Crowley, mid-hum, cranes her fleshy head around to see what's going on an instant before Hudson can duck away. Confused, Ms. Crowley drops the glass figurine to the floor. As she rises from the couch under old, malfunctioning legs and is prepared to scream for help, recognition ignites in her memory—*I know this boy!* In her haste to better see him she crucifies her bare foot on the glass bumblebee wing and pivots to the window. Ignoring the pain, she stares through the bars and witnesses the young man in flight.

After breakfast Nolan takes Speck to the lake for paddle boating. They drift so far out that returning is a strain on their legs. On shore Nolan takes Speck to lunch at a pizza parlor, and when they finish eating Nolan suggests frozen custard.

Now it is afternoon, and they are driving home. The windows are cranked since there's no air conditioning in the pickup. The wind drowns out conversation. Not that Speck has much to say; they've been talking all day. While the morning started out awkwardly at the diner (neither one of them wanted to bring up the confrontation with Hudson), by the time the check arrived the two had relaxed and could joke with one another. Speck did not know that Nolan had a sense of humor and was surprised when the man loosened the saltshaker so that the entire contents would dump out on the next customer who tried to season his home fries. And in the car Nolan let Speck choose the radio station. Speck couldn't find anything that he liked, so, instead, they discussed music. Nolan liked classic, and Speck admitted he liked classical. "You add those two letters *al* to the word and boy do you get a different tune," Nolan observed. Then in the boat on the lake Nolan talked about fishing—told tales—and struggled to recount times he took Hudson out. Speck listened and pedaled hard to keep up so that they didn't spin in circles. Afterwards, over pizza, Nolan said, "You watch, all that sun on your arms and legs will finish off that poison ivy by tomorrow."

Crunching along the graveled drive back at the vineyard, Nolan extends an arm to wave at Madison working the gift store. Speck nearly confesses that she and his brother have gotten together but he decides otherwise. The boy is already anxious about how things will play out between Nolan and Hudson, no need to get in the way.

When they are parked at the pink house Nolan keeps the engine running and turns to Speck before he has a chance to hop out. "I had a good time today," he says, squinting. He fumbles in his shirt pocket for a cigarette.

"You're not coming in?" Speck asks.

"I've got errands before my shift."

"All right," the boy says, stepping outside. By the road, midway into the field, Pepper breaks from one of the rows and lopes toward the house. "Can I ask you a question?"

Nolan tenses his face. He uses the circular lighter from the pickup to ignite his cigarette. "What?"

"You think Gus is okay?"

Nolan adjusts the rearview mirror so that he can see the old man's apartment. The blinds in the window are slightly bent. "Why do you ask?"

"I think I heard a gunshot last night."

"Well," Nolan shifts uncomfortably in the hot seat, "Sultan might not be okay."

"Why wouldn't he take the dog outside?"

"He's an old man."

"What did he do with the carcass?"

Before Nolan has a chance to answer Pepper suddenly jumps up to the driver's side window. "Jesus Christ," the man says, dropping his cigarette into his lap. "You scared the shit out of me, you mutt," Nolan says grabbing his cigarette. Pepper sticks his head into the window, and Nolan leans in to nuzzle. Scratching the dog's ears vigorously, he thinks nothing of the welts protruding from the dog's neck. For all he knows, welts this size are normal. Nolan has no way of knowing that three days ago a curious red fox was attacked by a small platoon of wasps that had advanced from the railroad. The dazed fox dizzily twirled to the vineyard where it died difficultly beneath the ripening fruit. The wasp hosts did what they do and then built a modest nest on the underside of a grape post near the cool, moist earth. The man has no way of knowing that this morning Pepper had been happily rolling around the fox remains when the rag-tag band of wasps attacked. The dog had been attacked before, and he was able to shake most of them off. What Nolan doesn't know is that a worker dropped a queen onto the dog's fur where it has been clinging and waiting to make her move. Nolan has no idea that leaning in so close to Pepper and scratching so hard will dislodge the queen and knock her onto his shirt collar.

"All right," Nolan swats Pepper down. The dog sprints around the pickup to the porch where he waits for the boy in the shade. "Listen, Gus is resourceful. If he did in fact put Sultan down—and that's a big if—he'll know how to dispose of it. Give him the benefit of the doubt."

Speck frowns. He rakes his nails up and down his chest.

Nolan suspects that the boy is going to ask more questions. Maybe something about Hudson. He checks his watch. It is almost four. This gives him about forty-five minutes before his shift starts—the perfect time to drink since it is not enough time to get drunk. Re-adjusting the mirror, he pulls away, leaving the boy in a small cloud of dust.

Once he's found his stool at Moonshadows and has a draft of pale ale he says, to the bartender, "Well, my son punched me in the face today."

Shane, the bartender, doing his job, asks, "What did you do?"

"Man," Nolan replies after drinking deeply. "I don't know. I'm rusty at being a dad."

Shane listens. He pours a second glass of beer and then a third. By that time, Nolan is done talking. He feels better. He's not such a bad dad, after all, as Shane suggests.

On a small television in the corner of the bar Nolan watches two women playing a game of pool. The patient queen who has been hiding beneath Nolan's shirt collar and waiting for the vibrations in her host's body to settle down—for Nolan to shut up—makes her move. She scuttles to the earlobe and then into the ear canal. What Nolan feels is a sharp pinch and then the sound from the television dims for a moment. He shakes his head and digs at his left ear with his fingernail. By now, though, it's too late. The queen is hunkered low, anchored by hooks extending from her abdomen while the egg sac—a droplet of acid honey—is sliding down. In a few moments she'll crawl out and die near a half-eaten bowl of peanuts.

Sound is dulled. Nolan holds his nose and tries to pop his ears. This, he thinks, helps. Draining his drink, checking his watch, shaking his head again, Nolan lifts a finger to Shane. He has time for one more.

15.

. . . five, four, three, two, one, and, zero. Hudson steps emphatically on the railroad tie he started from this morning. He took his time returning. By now, it is late afternoon. Shadows from the trees are lengthening. Finally, at rest, Hudson feels good. Hungry and thirsty, but good. He's had time to work some things through.

As he makes his way back through the forest Hudson is surprised how quiet things are. Without a breeze, the leaves aren't rustling. There is no birdsong or insect thrum. Hudson can hear the sounds of his footfalls and his even breathing and nothing else. He doesn't have much time to puzzle through this peculiarity before the road leading to the Muller houses picks up, and the white shepherd comes galloping out of a pool of shade to noisily greet him.

Back at the pink house Hudson finds his brother taking a nap in the bedroom. Speck's got one arm hanging off the bed, and he's wearing his earplugs. Hudson can faintly hear the music playing.

After he's done using the bathroom, Hudson cups water to his mouth from the sink and catches a glimpse of his face in the mirror. He is startled. His face is orange from the sun—on its way to red—and his split lip is having difficulty staying closed. His hair is standing out in wild patches where the sweat has dried and, as he gazes deeper, Hudson detects a hardness in his eyes that wasn't there a few days ago. He turns away and strips down for a cold shower.

Once he is clean, Hudson finds a pair of khaki shorts and a white T-shirt and dresses without waking his brother. On his way to the kitchen to find something to eat, Hudson catches a whiff of something foul. He stops and takes another deep breath. It is the scent of death rot, no mistake about it. He has smelled it many times before emanating from alleyways where wounded cats or pigeons have gone to die. Hudson furrows his brow, confused for a moment until it dawns on him that the raccoon from yesterday has probably given up the ghost. Kneeling, Hudson sniffs around the baseboard. The scent is fainter below. When he stands it is stronger as if it's coming from above.

Funny, Hudson thinks as he steps into the bathroom to find some cologne, *how scent travels*. He generously sprays the air in the hall before moving into the kitchen for food. It's strange eating with one less tooth. Once he has finished a sandwich and several cups of milk, he withdraws a piece of paper and pen. He writes:

> *Dad,*
>
> *I'm sorry for this morning. I never meant to get you involved. I see how busy you are, and the last thing I want to do is become a headache. Crowley can use the money he owes me for the last few days to pay for the broken taillight. That should easily cover it.*

Hudson puts the pen aside and a hand to his chin. He stares out the kitchen window. The note needs more, he knows. He should write, *When you defended Crowley it made me angry. You have no idea what kind of monster that man is. You do not want to side with him.* He also should write, *For so long it seems I have been on the receiving end of your neglect. And that's on you, not Mom. She's gone out of her way to let you be exactly who you are. And, Dad, I hate to admit that I really don't like who you are.*

Hudson is startled when he feels a hand on his shoulder—disengaged from his thoughts.

"Hey," Speck says.

"Hi," Hudson says, setting the pen down.

"I fell asleep."

"I noticed. You hungry? Want a sandwich?"

"I had pizza. What are you writing?"

"Nothing. Well, an apology."

"I think your dad's sorry, too," Speck says.

"What makes you say that?"

"He was really nice to me all day. I can't believe you slapped him."

"Did I leave a mark?"

"I don't think so." Speck cocks his head and flares his nostrils. "What stinks?"

"That coon in the bomb shelter below. You mind crawling down there and grabbing it?"

"Yeah, right."

"Just try to ignore it."

"All right. You know," the boy says as he runs the tips of his fingers along the countertop, "I was worried about you."

"I appreciate it, but stop. Things are going to change around here, I promise."

"Maybe we could take a walk tomorrow."

"Back into the woods?"

"Yeah. I'm willing to give it another shot."

"Well, I think that's a great idea," Hudson says, crumpling the note in his fist and tossing it into the trashcan. "Listen, I've got to do something tonight. You be all right if I go out for a while?"

"To see your girlfriend?"

Hudson grabs Speck and hoists him into his arms. "You're just jealous," he says as he kisses his brother's neck and cheeks.

Speck squirms away, protesting. He smiles and tries to smooth down his short hair.

"I'll be back soon." Hudson opens the front door.

Before he's gone Speck asks, "You in love?"

"Sure," Hudson replies. "Why the hell not?"

The post-rush hour traffic has dissipated on the highway. What remains are nighttime drivers pointing headlights to wherever. Nolan lights another cigarette. He has to momentarily let go of the wheel to do this. He holds his pickup steady and occasionally turns around to make sure the WIDE LOAD sign is properly fastened to the bed. The lumbering rig in front of him carries a MidLand trailer home that juts out into the passing lane. Nolan's job is to warn people too dumb enough to notice that there's a big vehicle hogging up the lanes in front of them. This way, MidLand avoids a messy lawsuit if there are any collisions. They turtle along, hugging the shoulder. It's not a bad job. Nolan has had plenty worse. One of the benefits is that you don't have to think. Or, you can think all you want.

Tonight, Nolan's mind is jumbled, and he's trying to puzzle through the day. The wind blowing through the open windows is so loud he has to crank the radio all the way up. Reed, the truck driver ahead of him, has a CB and can call Nolan if he has to. This happens rarely—what is there to say?—and Nolan couldn't hear it tonight anyway.

With a fierce twist Nolan shuts the radio off. "Well," he says, taking a drag and talking to an imagined version of his son riding shotgun, "I fucked up." With his pinky finger he roots around in his ear to try and clear out what's inside. "I'm out of practice. I probably should have planned on some things we could do. Maybe hike a trail or two. Go fishing. Catch a movie."

Outside the heat fades gradually. Anxious drivers ride Nolan's bumper, wait their turn, and then speed past the pickup and the trailer home, rolling over the rumble strips on the outside edge of the left lane. Everyone is in a hurry this time of night. People speeding past scowl at Nolan as if he were responsible for all the troubles in the world; he has caused them to move around, to *proceed with caution*, and they deeply resent it. Nolan doesn't meet their gazes. In fact, he prefers these hours when cars are still on the highway to the early a.m. desolation. Tonight the drop off point is in Amherst. It's a six-hour drive. Reed will leave the rig at the sister MidLand plant and then curl up in a blanket to sleep in the bed of the pickup while Nolan chauffeurs. They'll do it all again tomorrow—sometimes heading to the Wilkes-Barre site or the Hartford site or the East Stroudsburg site—so long as they don't break down. To get the salaried job, Nolan knows, he'll need a trucker's license but he's been dragging his feet not in a hurry to give up the routine he's already acquired.

"Maybe I'll call in sick tomorrow," he suggests to the Hudson who is not there. Prior to the visit Nolan has often pretended his son was sitting by his side. It's a way of practicing for the real thing. "Then again, what kind of message does that send? You can't just go and do whatever you want whenever you want to. Which was my point this morning."

The Hudson buckled in beside him listens attentively.

"A man earns his keep by punching in, doing his job, and punching out. That's about the only truth I know so it's the best advice I can offer. All the stuff with the heart . . . I'm not so good at that."

And although his ear is clogged, and the heavy-dull roar of the wind is whipping through the cab he can hear his imagined son reply, "Yes you are, Dad," without an ounce of sarcasm.

Hudson slips a bottle of red wine, a blanket, a hammer, a flashlight, and an extra pair of sneakers into his backpack and leaves at twilight with the promise of returning soon.

Once his brother is gone, Speck spends some time on the computer with his video game. Then, curious, he does a little more research on wasps. There's plenty to learn. When he's read enough he plunks down on the couch in the den and cracks the journal open. There is something familiar about the world in the diary that he just can't quite pin down. There's a thrill in thinking that the book has been written, somehow, specifically for him to read. So, he continues:

Monday, June 24: 20:30

What a day. I thought about calling you to let you know that I'm on my way. Almost did. But then I'd ruin the surprise, and I really can't wait to see the look on your face when I walk through the door.

I thought I'd have a chance to relax a little now that I'm on board. I was completely wrong about that. It was somehow easier back in the jungle. The problem is Willy. He has changed. Last night I couldn't sleep. Too excited, I guess. Finally, I did drift off. I don't know how long I was out but when I woke up we were moving. It was dark with a sliver of light squeezing in through the porthole. In that semi-dark I saw Tolly holding Willy's cage aloft and rattling it. For a moment, I thought I was still asleep. I slid off the cot to see what was going on. Tolly said he was making sure the monkey hadn't died. I could smell that Tolly had been drinking; his words were slurred. The sailors had drowned him.

Without much light, I couldn't tell if Willy was breathing or not. When I leaned close, though, the little guy opened his eyes, which were bloodshot and wild, and then he bared his teeth and reached one of his hands out of the cage. I managed to jump aside, but Tolly wasn't quick enough. Willy raked his nails down Tolly's forearm. Scratched him good and deep. Later, I'd tease Tolly, looked like he lost a fight with a teenage girl. Anyway, Tolly dropped the cage and cursed. I don't know which part of all this set Willy off, but the creature started to howl and scream and freak out. I tried to take charge of the situation. I righted the cage, turned the lights on, guided Tolly to a chair, and rooted out some peroxide for the wounds. You could see three bright-red lines tattooed on the underside of his arm. He said it didn't hurt, which made sense, and it was easy to clean him up and guide him to his cot where he could pass out. Willy, though, wouldn't let anyone else sleep. He kept screaming and bouncing around in that makeshift cage and nothing I did could get him to quit. Went on all night. Several sailors complained. I hadn't been on board more than a dozen hours, and I had already pissed people off. Bruised and beaten by his thrashing Willy finally wore himself down enough for me to catch a couple hours of sleep before rising with the dawn to clean toilets all morning and then, because I'm a pal, doubled my duties and covered for Tolly who needed to recover. He wasn't able to act like a human until late in the afternoon. He thanked me profusely. I asked him what he thought was wrong with Willy. He told me monkeys don't like water.

Wonderful.

I've been dragging all day. Haven't had a chance to lift my head high enough to look outside. Hell, I'll do it now. All right. The sun's down. The sky and water are steel blue. Tolly's dozing. Willy's watching me write. Maybe something about the way I'm moving my pen interests him. Here you go, little fellow, write down what you're thinking.

Monday, June 24: I don't know the exact time—
maybe 3 or 4 in the morning.

I'm trying to be quiet now. I woke up a few minutes ago from a bad dream. When I looked over at Willy he was still watching me with these deadpan eyes. I don't think he's blinked all night. It's pretty creepy. Maybe monkeys can see in the dark? I can hear Tolly snoring in his sleep. The waves are making that sound that waves make against the ship. Otherwise, it's quiet. Willy's kind of smiling, I think, or else grimacing. His legs are tucked behind him, and his arms are dangling loosely between the bars. For some reason, and I know this sounds crazy, I suspect that he's somehow responsible for my nightmares. Like he has somehow gotten into my head and is messing around. I turned the cage around, but he just rearranged himself so that he was peering at me again. I don't know what he's got against me. I reminded him that I'm the one who rescued him. Doesn't seem to matter.

I'll just put him in the closet and try to get some sleep.

Tuesday, June 25: 21:00

Have you ever noticed how, when you're on the verge of escaping someplace, life just won't let you go? Like misjudging the surface when you're coming up for air. Or, like having something hold your leg so you can't rise. I feel like I'm drowning, I guess.

After I returned from morning duties I opened the closet to check on Willy, and I found him dead. Make no mistake about it; he was dead. It looked like he bashed his brains out. His fingers were bloody from picking at his eyes and ears with a kind of insane fury. There was vomit and feces smeared all over, and his body was twisted the wrong way. His eyes had popped out of his sockets, and his mouth was agape. At first I thought he'd gotten into a bowl of oatmeal with raisins until I realized that he'd gnashed his tongue to bits. Should probably spare you the details, but it helps to get it out of my head and onto the page.

I found Tolly polishing brass on deck. He was in shock, too. Together, we tried to figure out what happened. The lock on the cage hadn't been disturbed so there's no way anyone could have snuck into the cabin and done this to him. Willy had done it to himself. I guess he just went mad. This, of course, made Tolly concerned about the scratches on his arm. If the monkey was diseased, Tolly might need medical attention. He scampered off to the infirmary.

I finished my duties and am done for the night. There's a storm rocking us around. I feel nauseous and exhausted. Hard to even hold this pen. I wish I could sleep, but every time I put my head down I think of Willy either staring at me last night or else imagining his decomposing body in the closet.

What I should do is thank that damned monkey. I wouldn't be here now without him. I'll try to appreciate the sacrifice he made and not think of him as he is now in the closet.

Wednesday, June 26: 05:50

Tolly returned last night with a large cooler full of ice. He's been given a shot of penicillin and is required to see a doctor when we're home. We're going to try and preserve the body so that scientists can perform an autopsy. I helped pack Willy in and sealed the cooler with duct tape. It was some stench. We pitched the cage and are airing out the closet. I washed my hands for five full minutes.

While we've passed through the storm I'm still feeling nauseous. I'm hoping a hard day of work will settle me.

Thursday, June 27: 19:00

That storm I mentioned yesterday had another one trailing it. Slow going. We'll be delayed by at least a day. Right now we're in the middle of nowhere. If we went down we'd never be found. This journal would wash ashore in China, and people wouldn't be able to make heads or tails out of it. Flipping back, it's amazing how many pages I've scribbled. All because of you.

Tolly plays poker with a group of guys, and I don't see him much. I suspect I won't ever see him again once we hit shore. (First I'll make him buy me that drink he promised.) I've never been good at keeping friends.

My stomach is a little better. I borrowed a book about baseball from one of the cooks, but every time I try to read it I get motion sickness. Even writing in this makes me queasy. I've either got to find my sea legs or else grow bigger balls. Either way, I'm going to quit bitching.

Speck sets the book down in his lap when he hears footsteps outside on the stairs to Gus's apartment. The boy freezes. By now it is dark. It occurs to him that he has been squinting at the pages. He cannot determine if someone is walking up the steps or else coming down. He hopes it is the old man, but he dismisses the thought; Gus wouldn't be able to move this fast.

The cell phone is on the nightstand. Speck regards it with disdain. Who is he going to call, and what will he say? That he hears a noise and maybe there's somebody outside walking around or maybe it's nobody, just a trick of the mind? The truth is that he's alone with his imagination and dread. He wishes he could tell Gent, wherever he is right now, that he's scared. That he knows, he can just feel it, that something terrible is about to unravel. He'd ask the soldier to march outside and illuminate the night, beat back the shadows.

16.

Prowling around the outside of the house Hudson finds a light on in Madison's bedroom. He scoops up a few clods of dirt and tosses them, with success, at her window. After a few moments the mini-blinds lift, the window opens, and Madison squints down. When she sees Hudson she smiles. "Ever hear of a front door?"

"I'm a romantic," Hudson whispers loudly.

"My Romeo."

"Something like that," Hudson says. "Get down here, Juliet. Let's go on an adventure."

As he makes his way to the front of the house the last of the evening light cascades at Hudson's feet. He can feel the ache in his calves from walking the rail all day, the sunburn pulses against the back of his neck, and the faint taste of blood still lingers where his tooth had been, but he feels awake and sharp and fine, fine, fine.

When Madison steps out of the house and approaches wearing jeans and a thin, red, short-sleeve shirt, Hudson's heart rolls. He says, "The sun has been waiting all day to cast you in the last of its light."

Madison shakes her head and gives Hudson a quick kiss. "All right, Shakespeare. What did you have in mind?"

Hudson takes Madison's hand and pulls her into a skip down the road toward the woods. "I've got something I want to show you."

Mid-way down the path Pepper tears away from his spot on the porch at the pink house—a ghostly flash—to garner attention from the couple. Madison smoothes the dog's ears and pats his back, and then they continue on. In the dark it is difficult to tell that the roses in the bushes at the ends of the rows—meant to attract bugs away from the grapes—are all dead. They've been ravished by the wasps.

At the end of the road, near the automobile cemetery, where the forest begins, Pepper hesitates. He whines and lowers himself with his forelegs flat to the ground.

"What's with him?" Hudson asks.

"I don't know," Madison says. She tries to coax the dog forward by calling his name softly. Pepper continues to whine and walks around in two, tight circles before barking and turning back to the house.

"I guess you just lost your chaperone," Hudson says, removing a flashlight from his backpack and flipping it on.

Madison laughs. "These are my woods. I could find my way blindfolded. I highly doubt you're going to show me something I haven't seen back here."

"We'll see," Hudson says, plunging ahead. Behind the curving light he leads them single file along the path he has walked before. "Since you're such an expert, maybe you could tell me why it's so quiet out here."

Madison shakes her head. "Don't know. Maybe it's not quiet, you're just loud."

"You want to take the lead here?"

"Nope," she says, smacking him in the ass, "you're doing just fine."

In a moment, the woods relent, and they're at the railroad. Hudson scampers up to stand on one of the ties. The glow of the flashlight disappears in the vast expanse of tracks. "That way leads back home."

Madison untangles a twig from her hair. She's not wearing the right shoes for a hike.

"You ever think about hopping one?" Hudson asks.

"Not really," she says, walking to stand by his side. She pulls a cigarette from her pack and lights up. "You want one?"

"Believe it or not, I've never smoked."

"I believe it," Madison says. "Here," she puts the cigarette to his lips, "take a quick breath."

Hudson inhales the smoke and holds it in his mouth. It comes burning out his nose and, coughing and laughing, he shakes his head. "The country girl is corrupting the city boy," Madison teases.

"Hardly. Why don't you come visit me sometime?"

Madison is caught off guard by the question. She stays tight-lipped and narrows her eyes at Hudson.

Not sure how to read her response, Hudson says, "We could just walk. Take a day or so. I wonder how many ties there are from here to Penn Station?"

"You know how my grandfather would answer that question?"

"How?"

"All of them."

Hudson groans. "That's bad." He points the flashlight into the woods on the other side of the tracks. "We're not going that way tonight."

Madison takes a long drag and casts the cigarette into the scruff before following. The two make their way down to the river and the rope swing. Hudson came this way to avoid the wasps he knows are further up river. He has no intention of disturbing them ever again. Around a small bend not far from the rope swing—Hudson noticed it days ago when he was up in the tree—the water narrows. He rolls his pant legs around his knees

"I'm not sure what you have in mind here, but if it's skinny dipping, count me out."

"Nah," Hudson says. Before she can react he bends low and cradles her in his arms. "I'm carrying you across."

The moon overhead stains the water in a break through the trees. Hudson splashes across appreciating how tightly Madison is clinging to him. She is smiling and happy and mid-way across he kisses her, and once they are across he kisses her some more.

"You should have taken off your shoes, dummy," Madison says gazing down at the puddle of mud Hudson has made.

"I brought an extra pair," he says, patting his backpack. He grabs her hand. "Come on. We're almost there."

On the other side of the stream the trees begin to thin, and the Summerfield development begins. Hudson leads her into the backyard of the house he has been working with Crowley. It is dark enough to see a blanket of stars overhead. "This," Hudson says extending his arms as if he has discovered the sky, "is something, isn't it?"

Madison is slightly winded. She lets her arms dangle at her side and blows a few strands of hair away. She's surprised that he hasn't noticed that she isn't wearing her bracelets anymore, and her tattoo is exposed for all to see. She is, in fact, disappointed that her mother hasn't noticed, either. She gazes down at the dirt they are standing in and says, "No. It's an unfinished yard behind an unfinished house in an unfinished neighborhood. More ugly suburban sprawl."

Ignoring her, Hudson sweeps his arms in a wide arc across the backyard. "I'd put a fence along the border and a deck by the house, maybe a Jacuzzi, and a grill over there, and plants—what kind of flowers do you like?—daffodils and maybe some roses like the ones you've already got, if you like, and we could plant a few elm trees along the fence line to give the forest perspective so that, when they get big enough we could fasten a hammock between them and float away."

"We?" Madison asks.

"Well not *us* exactly, but the idea of us, maybe."

"God," Madison says, putting her arms around his shoulders, "you're hopeless."

"I know," he says tugging at her jeans as he walks backwards toward the sliding glass door. "Let me show you inside."

Speck cautiously stands and creeps into the living room and the mantle where he can hide the book inside the butterfly box. Then he remains still. The footfalls have stopped outside the front door, and whoever is standing there is waiting for something. The boy can feel the presence of the other person poised just on the other side. Though he expects it, the suddenness of the knock makes him jump. He waits several seconds to collect himself before turning the handle and peering out.

"Hi," Clara says when she sees the boy through the crack. She has her hands on her hips and is unsmiling. Her hair is pinned tightly back in a clip. She is wearing a long, blue, sundress that falls loosely around her thin frame. Speck wonders why she's wearing lipstick at this hour. He studies her painted red nails.

"Hello, Ms. Muller." He opens the door wide.

"Has Madison been over here tonight?"

"No."

"Your dad?"

"He's at work. And he's not my . . ."

"Brother?"

"He was here earlier." Speck fights the urge to scratch his chest and legs, his whole body. If only he could convince this woman to take her tantalizing fingernails and rake them across his desperate skin. "Do you want to come in?"

"Yes," Clara pushes past Speck, arms crossed, and into the house. "It stinks."

"I forgot," the boy says, standing sheepishly aside.

Clara studies the apartment wordlessly. Her penetrating scrutiny intimidates the boy, and his nail-scratching fantasy evaporates. He moves his attention from her nails to her vibrantly bright lips.

"When did you last see my father?"

Under her gaze, Speck snaps to attention. "Last night."

"What was his temperament?"

"I would say unusual, Ms. Muller."

"Elaborate."

"He was really happy. Perhaps giddy?"

"Be more specific."

"I think he shot the dog."

Clara's eyes dart back and forth, analyzing the boy. "Evidence?"

"Well, the smell."

"Right."

"And I think I heard something last night."

"Listen, kid . . ."

"It's Speck."

" . . . thinking you heard something is not helpful. Be clear."

"A gunshot," Speck says, exasperated. He feels perspiration rising out of every pore. "Maybe it was nothing."

Clara stamps her foot, says, "Wait here."

"I told Mr. Baxter," Speck says as she rushes by, leaving the front door open. The boy counts the footsteps up the stairs—one, two, three, four . . . He hears her knock and then call out. There is silence. Speck watches the empty space the front door leaves. Upstairs, Clara is jiggling the handle. The boy suddenly recollects that he was standing right where he is standing now this morning.

Clara's footfalls on the stairs coming down are rushed. Speck cannot count them all. She may have skipped a few. For an instant, like a blink, she occupies the space of the front door. Then she whisks by, muttering, "I left my keys at the house; your father keeps a spare in his bedroom . . ." sliding around Speck as if he were a piece of furniture. She's not in

Nolan's room long—nearly flying now with a key clutched tightly in her fist—glancing off the boy on her way out and then up the stairs again. She's fumbling with the lock to Gus's apartment. Speck feels something building here. It's not unlike a few days ago the way he anticipated that Pepper would bark, and the wasps would descend. It's not unlike the moment when the boy was on the sidewalk and turned to witness the bicyclist get swiped by the taxi. He recognizes the terrible electricity in the air.

Speck hears the upstairs door creak open and then bang against the inside wall. Then it is quiet. Clara hasn't moved. He scratches the underside of his neck, unblinking. When he finally hears Clara make a loud, shrill sound, he thinks it is some kind of weird laughter. Then, as the fine hairs on the back of his neck rise, he understands that she is screaming.

Afterwards, Madison and Hudson eventually dress. For a while the two stayed tucked into the thick blanket Hudson brought for them drinking wine and talking in the soft glow of the flashlight.

"This house has been christened," Madison says.

"There are a half-dozen others waiting for us."

After slipping through the unlocked sliding glass door the two ended up on the floor in the family room surrounded by the newly hung drywall and dust. Hudson has had to battle back the urge to sneeze.

"To think," Madison says as she slides her shirt on, "the owners will have no idea we were here."

Hudson takes a pull from the wine bottle and feels himself getting light-headed. "That's exactly right." He roots around in his backpack and withdraws the hammer.

"What's that?" Madison says, surprised. Up until now it's been pretty easy to read him, and she's been enjoying doing so. "You going to do some work?"

"No," Hudson says, rising unsteadily to his feet. He swaggers into the foyer twirling the hammer like a baton. "I'm going to undo it." He smashes the hammer into the wall.

"Hey," Madison says, "what are you doing?" She trains the flashlight on him. "You're drunk, aren't you?"

Hudson removes the head of the hammer from the wall and goes at it with the claw-end. He gives himself over to the demolition creating a hole the size of a tire in no time.

"Hudson," Madison shouts over the commotion, "stop it!"

Satisfied and breathing heavily, Hudson reaches his arm into the darkness and finds what he came for. Turning back to Madison, he has to lower his eyes from the light. "Look at this." He holds the glass crocodile up so that it glitters in the shine.

"What is it?"

Hudson walks forward excitedly. "It's a crocodile. Crowley has been stealing them from his mother and walling them into these houses. She's got a ton of glass animals, but he only takes the ones his dead brother gave her. And then," Hudson continues, wild-eyed, "he gets a tattoo done. He's going to strap his mom into her wheelchair and do a striptease in front of her. Isn't that fucked up?"

Madison takes a step back, spooked. "How do you know all this?"

"I've been to their place. I was there today. Saw his mom. That old woman's messed up in the head."

"Don't say that," Madison says, anger flaring.

"I don't mean it like that," Hudson backpedals. "I think she's lonely. She needs help."

"You're the knight in shining armor?"

"I'm just returning what he stole from her. What's wrong with that?"

"That's not why you're doing this."

"Well, don't cry for Crowley. You know what an asshole he is. I thought you'd appreciate what I'm doing."

"Is this why you brought me out here?"

"No," Hudson says, reaching forward to touch Madison's elbow. He's still holding the hammer, and he realizes that she might misread the gesture. He drops it to the ground and tries again. "I wanted to be with you."

Madison backs away. "I don't want any part of this."

"Come on," Hudson tries, "don't be like that."

"Leave me alone," she says. "I'm going back."

"I'll come with you."

"No way. Here," she says underhanding the flashlight. The light loops in a wide circle. It is too disorienting for Hudson to follow. It crashes at his feet and dies. "I don't need this."

Alone, in the dark, Hudson tries to find his bearings. This isn't how he intended the evening to unfold. He shouldn't have gotten her involved.

He's not exactly sure how to undo what he's done here, and he's not sure that he wants to.

"All right," he says to the crocodile. "We'll let fate decide." He bends down to find the flashlight. "If this thing is broken, I'll chase after her and apologize. But if it's not, you and I are going to go rescue your brothers. Sound good?"

The happy crocodile doesn't care.

Pointing the flashlight at the figurine in his palm, Hudson counts: "One, two, three." He flips the switch. Light blooms and illuminates the crocodile. It's like the young man is cupping a star.

Speck remembers to breathe. He lets air out and then sucks it back in. Shortly after the scream dissipates the boy hears a dragging sound from above and a series of thumps descending the stairs. Reluctantly, on puppet strings, he takes two difficult steps onto the porch.

Clara has her arms tucked under Gus's armpits. Speck pinpoints the red of her nails as he clutches the old man to her chest. She drags his body down the stairs. One of his house slippers slides off a foot and teeters at the edge of a step. When she gets to the landing she does not notice Speck. Still muttering, she continues down the porch steps. What's left of Gus's face and head—the unforgiving remains from the bullet as it traveled from one ear to the other—bobs against his floppy neck as if in affirmation to a question the boy didn't ask—*Yes, yes, yes.*

Speck turns away and resists the urge to sprint to bed and cower under covers. He holds his head in his hands and pinches his eyes shut; *Perhaps this is just a dream?* When he opens them again he follows the faint trail of parallel lines Gus's feet are leaving in the dirt down to where Clara is struggling to open the hangar door. The boy has no idea what she's doing. Before he can figure it out, he is distracted by a piece of paper on the bottom step. It's a note, apparently written by Gus, which must have slipped out of the old man's pocket. It reads, in messy cursive, *Raze the fields.* The boy has no idea what this means. He slides the paper into his sock and tells himself he'll show it to Clara later. Then he catches a whiff of the foul stench coming from Gus's apartment. He casts his eyes up the stairs and into the mouth of the doorway. For a second, his brain cannot make sense of what he sees—fingers of smoke spiraling out into the night sky. It's too dark inside for there to be a fire. Well before he hears the low, buzzing thrum emanating from the escaping insects and the haze of his confusion lifts, Speck recognizes the wasps rising away.

When Nolan's cell phone rings around two in the morning—the call is from his son who is frantic and wants to explain that Gus killed himself and that Clara situated the body into the cockpit of the B-26 in the barn insisting that her father needed to be close to her mother and that the authorities are on the scene verifying that what happened is as obvious as it seems (although they do find it difficult to explain why Sultan's body has been so severely ravaged, the dog's skull exposed in places where the skin had been worn away), another suicide in the Muller family, and yes, there is a bit of a wasp infestation, they must have gotten in through a crack in the roof . . . , so when Hudson is instructed by his cordial, familiar, automated-father's voice to leave a message after the beep, the young man says, his voice cracking, "Dad, there's been an incident," and nothing more—Nolan does not hear it.

In the truck bed Reed slumbers. Nolan is chain-smoking, and when he finishes his third-to-last cigarette he lets out a growl. There are still two more hours to go, and there's no way he can stretch what's left in the pack all the way. He doesn't need gas and does not need to pee and really just wants to get into bed and wake up tomorrow without this migraine that has settled upon him like a crown of thorns and start all over with his son.

The rumble strips along the side of the road warn Nolan that he is heading into the ditch. He straightens himself, checks to see that Reed is still asleep, and shakes his head. To stay awake, he continues the conversation with his imaginary son in the passenger seat. "If I could go back, I would. I'd see it through for you. We'd have spent time with your grandfather out on the lake. Your mom and I would have given you a brother. I'd take you to Yankees games." When he speaks out loud his voice sounds far-off and muted. "I was in line for a raise. You might not know it, but I can be a people person when I want to. I could have made a little money—not as much as your stepfather, but we'd make do . . ." Nolan steers the pickup into his lane to correct the drift. "My balance is off," he says. "Your old man may have lost a step. I can still stand with the best of them. Maybe I'll buy some gloves so we can spar in the barn. Next time you hit me, I'll hit you back."

17.

Farmers use wasps to control pests. Citrus growers in California import a tiny parasitic wasp—half the size of a chocolate sprinkle—from Pakistan to attack psyllids which spread a disease that makes oranges lumpy and bitter. The female wasp lays an egg in the belly of the psyllid, and when it hatches, it feasts upon the host.

Some vintners use Muscidifurax raptor to fight fruit flies in vineyards. The wasps inject their eggs through an ovipositor into the fruit fly larvae along with venom that compromises the immune system. Once the fly larvae defenses have been incapacitated, the wasp larvae use sharp appendages to tear and devour from the inside out. The parasites save the brain and eyes for last.

The sun crests over the trees and bathes the vineyard in light and heat. This early in the season the grapes are pea-sized and clustered together like ordinary fruit. In a couple of months they will ripen and take on distinctive varieties. Each orb will stretch its flesh and test the limits of the bunch—seek to snap from the little community on the vine. It is difficult to stave off the curious desire to detach. There is no need to give this much thought. The harvest comes sooner than you expect. They will be plucked and pulverized, blended into the essence of the others—aged and bottled until the beauty of individual shape and dimension is replaced by classifiable specifications of flavor and body and aftertaste. Grapes in the vineyard are merely a means to an end at the bottom of a glass.

There will be grapes that are overlooked. It is inevitable. Some will be spared by the harvesters. Eventually weight will overcome the strength of the wilting stalk trying to hold the bunch together and a renegade grape will unexpectedly find itself free on the earth. The wind will blow, and the outcast will roll. There is a thrill to the adventure. Who knows what exists in the next row? A bit of bruising is a reasonable price to pay for a peek over the horizon. In time, all wanderers must settle. That robust skin will sag and shrivel. Things will sour. And as months pass and the cold earth claims the tired remains, will the grape remember the sweet times huddling in the bunch? If given the choice, would it be worth the sacrifice to go back and feel the glorious crush with the others?

Beyond the field, sunlight finds the Muller estate like it always does. Standing on the porch last night Speck made the decision to call 911 instead of hiding under his covers. Better that he call for help than follow Clara into the hangar. No need for the boy to witness Clara's meltdown, the way the woman crammed her father's frame into the cockpit and sealed him in. The old man's damaged body suffered further trauma. Speck did not need to hear Clara humming as she rocked herself back and forth beneath the propeller until the police arrived.

After hanging up, Speck called his mother. He hoped to hear her concerned voice to balance the wildness in Clara's. As he expected, though, he was directed to voicemail. He didn't leave a message. Instead, he fidgeted there on the porch and watched the world from a remove. First came the cops in cars with whirling lights. They told the boy to step aside. One team of officers entered Gus's apartment while another investigated the barn. Then an ambulance and a fire engine arrived. All the lights were like the grand finale of a Fourth of July show. Everybody acted like they had seen this all before, no great mystery here. An EMT put a blanket around Clara's defeated shoulders, even though it was still quite hot, and coaxed her into sipping from a bottle of water.

Speck wondered if anyone was going to ask him any questions. He kept waiting for the right time to show someone Gus's curious suicide note. Since nobody asked, he left it in his sock.

The boy would have liked to offer his opinion on the recent events. While he didn't know everything that was going on he did know the journal he was reading might shed some light. The wasps in the book seemed like the same wasps that were in the woods and in Gus's apartment. If someone would only ask, the boy could explain that the insects were making people and animals go mad.

Down by the hanger he saw Madison. Hudson was not with her. She stood close to her mother trying to hold her upright. Clara seemed to be crumpling under the blanket, diminishing, melting into the dirt. Speck's eyes grew accustomed to the strobe lights. He made measured and deliberate blinks. Paramedics loaded Clara inside an ambulance and carted her to the hospital. Madison hurried to her car to follow.

Finally, Hudson came home, slinking through the trees to consult with the teeming authorities gathered by the barn. He marched right up to Speck and embraced him. In his brother's arms, the boy broke down. He shook and sobbed until Hudson carried him inside and rocked him to sleep.

Shortly after the sun finds the pink house, Speck wakes up. The first thing he notices is that he does not feel the urge to scratch his skin off. The poison ivy is beginning to fade. This is the first good sign he has seen in a while. With that slight slice of optimism Speck dresses. He retrieves Gus's note from the discarded sock in his dirty pile of laundry on the floor and puts it into his back pocket.

Hudson is sleeping and does not awaken despite the noise the boy makes. His brother is still dressed in the T-shirt and shorts he wore last night. At the foot of the bed rests the backpack. Speck can see a wet pair of sneakers sticking out. Speck wonders what Hudson was doing out in the woods so late last night. He hasn't the slightest clue. The boy begrudgingly acknowledges that his brother is turning into a stranger.

Speck exits the room and makes his way into the hall. Because the door to the bathroom is cracked he pushes it open and begins to enter. Inside, Nolan is leaning over the sink so that his face is an inch from the mirror. He has a pair of thin scissors poised inches from his ear.

"Oh," Speck says.

"What did I tell you?" Nolan shouts through clenched teeth at the boy's reflection in the mirror. He swivels in a gathering rage. "Knock first."

Speck falls back as the door slams in his face. He stumbles into the living room, his heart racing. The boy was considering showing Mr. Baxter Gus's note and asking the man when he thought it would be a good time to show to Clara.

On second thought, it might be best to let the man be. His nerves seem frayed just like so many other adults around here. Better just keep quiet and wait for the right opportunity to present itself.

Surveying the room, Speck remembers the journal. It's still in the box on the mantle where he left it. There really isn't much left. He moves into the den and sits on the sofa. He's eager to get to the end. At the same time, he feels a stab of sadness knowing that it will be over.

Friday, June 28: 06:00

Didn't sleep much last night. Huge surprise. About the time I got deep in Tolly woke me with all his drunken blundering. Am losing my patience.

Friday, June 28: 18:30

Another day done. More and more rain outside. We've got to be home soon. I don't know how sailors can do it. Lake Ontario's got big enough waves for me. Give me pinecones and whirligigs. Icicles and scarecrows. Hell, I'd even square dance. Know any pretty girls?

Saturday, June 29: 07:45

This time I can't blame Tolly. I woke up because I felt something on my face. The first thing I thought of was Willy. He must have been in my dreams stretching out his bony fingers, clawing me. I flipped on the light and scoured the room. Nothing. Somehow, I managed to fall back asleep. Must have slept on my elbow or something because my ear is clogged.

Saturday, June 29: 17:25

Just after dinner I returned to our cabin and found it in chaos. Tolly and a few of the sailors were inside and running around with a broom and spraying the place with insecticide. There were wasps in our room. They had made a small nest in our closet. Tolly thought they might have flown in through the window. That seems unlikely to me, but I suppose they could have been on some driftwood floating by.

The thing is, and I mentioned this to Tolly, the insects sort of resembled those nasty-looking wasps I saw back in Nuristan. They were mashed up and swept away before I could confirm it. Tolly frowned at me skeptically. I don't much appreciate that look.

Sunday, June 30: 06:25

If I hadn't sworn off bitching I'd tell you all about this wicked headache I have. I keep hearing tiny squishing sounds. Maybe it has something to do with being out on the ocean. Does that make any sense?

Sunday, June 30: 23:00

I can see the lights. We've made good time and are set to dock in about an hour. If I play my cards right, I'll be able to spend the Fourth with you! All my stuff is packed and ready to go. Everything, including me, will need to be processed and combed over. Including this journal. I'm cutting out now so I can get this to the authorities. This will be my final entry. I love you so much, Kylie. Every time I've written in this thing I've imagined you. It's not the real thing, but it's better than nothing.

Over and out.

Your loving brother,

Bill

Monday, July 1: 20:50

I was wrong. It's not over. I am out, though. All clear. Somehow, I passed all their tests. I must have put on a convincing acting job because I feel like shit. Maybe this is how I'm supposed to look. Maybe this is how I'm supposed to feel. We all watched a video about transitioning from soldier to citizen, but I was too distracted to pay much attention. When I get home I'll see a doctor.

Right now I'm at the train station slouched against the wall. People passing by keep giving me this look—just a look, you know, like I've done something wrong. The thing is, Kylie, those strangers are right. I have done bad things. I've just kept them to myself and kept them out of this journal since I knew I'd be screened. Well, I'm free to write what I want now.

What I want to tell you—what I need to tell someone—is why I enlisted. Only Dad and the sheriff know, and I suspect they've kept quiet. Before I get into that, let me tell you what happened once I left the dock. It was pretty late, and I ended up taking a rain check on that drink Tolly owes me so I started walking to the station. I've grown spoiled having a tracker with me, and I ended up getting turned around. I eventually found train tracks and followed them. Right away, a group of guys—kids really—started hassling me. I'm still in uniform and I guess this seemed funny to them. They kept calling me "Sir." Like, "Give me all your money, Sir." And then they'd laugh like crazy. Still laughing, one guy shoved me, and another guy tried to steal my pack, and, Kylie, I just lost it. It's hard for me to remember the particulars. I remember they had knives. There weren't any guns. The one day I'm unarmed I'm attacked. How do you like that? Anyway, I knocked the knives away and flew into a rage. I'd be lying if I didn't tell you that it felt good to take all the pent up pain in my head and share it with them.

The problem is I couldn't stop. One guy managed to run off, but I beat the other two severely. No doubt, even with this pounding headache and swollen knuckles, I'm better off than they are.

That's not what I wanted to confess here, though. I lied to you and everyone else when I told you that the Army recruited me because of my sharp-shooting skills. It's true, that's how I've served, but nobody ever contacted me. Dad's the one who made the call and, with help from the sheriff, they sent me off and swept the truth under the rug. The truth is that I was in the woods with Phil and Brian in the middle of January hanging out in our old tree fort like we always did. Drinking and smoking and just being dumb. It had been snowing for several days, and we'd been cooped up. I had my rifle, and we were passing it around. We built a half-dozen snowmen and took turns sniping them from the tree house. Phil brought a bag of charcoal, and he gave the snowmen eyes. That's what we were aiming for. Those boys were lucky if they could even hit the head. Me, I was shooting their pupils out.

I was probably guilty of bragging. I never learned how to hold my tongue once I'd had a few. Those guys ganged up on me. They admitted I was better than them, but that they'd seen Vince—you remember that guy; he graduated a few years ahead of me and was always kind of quiet—skeet shooting out in the cornfield. Vince could hit a moving target with ease, apparently.

I said I could, too. We climbed down from our fort, Phil grabbed the bag of charcoal, and we walked to the edge of the woods out by the county road. Brian and Phil took turns chucking charcoal into the bleak winter sky. My aim wasn't so good. In fairness, it was getting dark and my hands were numb. I'd only nick one out of every three they threw. So, they proved their point. I was a little pissed so I decided to hang back when they took off. I wanted to prove to myself that I was better than Vince. With Brian and Phil gone, I started searching for birds. I scared a flock of crows out of a tree and nailed one mid-flight. It spiraled down to the forest floor and lay there twitching at my feet, staining the snow red. I watched its life drain away. Sometimes I wonder if that senseless killing somehow caused me to do what I did next. Like, maybe something sinister rose up out of the dying bird's spirit and entered my head. Crazy, I know. But I have no other way to explain why, when I lifted my head and saw a silver car chugging down the county road, I raised the rifle, took quick aim at the front driver's side tire and fired. The car must have been one hundred yards away, and the car was driving around fifty miles per hour. Do you have any idea how slim the odds are of even the most skilled sharpshooter hitting that target under the best of conditions? One in a million. And I've wished a million times I could take it all back.

At first, I thought I'd missed. Nothing happened. I lowered the gun and was prepared to head home. Then, the car swerved off the road and rolled into the ditch. One second it was moving along the horizon and the next it was just gone. I remember how, for a split-second, everything was quiet and calm. Some snow was still shaking out of the tree where the crows had roosted. There weren't any other cars on the road. It was just still. I remember wondering if what had just happened hadn't really happened. I wonder how different my life would have been if I pretended that I hadn't been there and walked away. What kind of man I would have turned into.

Anyway, I ran over to the car. It was Mr. McCormick, the high school librarian. You, and everyone else, were told that he hit a patch of black ice and skidded off the road. Now you know the truth. If Dad wasn't such close friends with the sheriff, I'd have done some time. Sometimes I wish I had. Instead, they covered it up, and off I went. And here I am now. Every day I pray that Mr. McCormick came out of that coma. I have faith that he did. He woke up a better man, somehow. He has been kinder to his wife, to his children, to the kids at

school. He has had the chance to finish all the books he'd been mean-
ing to read. He's able to appreciate a sunset differently. That's what I
want to believe, and I'm convinced that if I concentrate hard enough,
it'll be true.

I guess I'll find out soon enough.

Monday? Night.

I'm on the train. My head is on fire. I'm trying so hard not to lose
my shit. When I look outside, I feel nauseous. I have this desire to
hurt someone again. To divert the pain.

This woman in the seat in front of me keeps whispering to her kid
and glancing back at me nervously. I can't hear what she's saying. She
keeps wiggling her hands in front of the child. It's some kind of code I
can't figure out.

I have no idea where I am. It might not even be Monday. I've
been drifting in and out. Everything is spinning. When I'm under,
I keep picturing Willy ripping off his face. When I'm awake, all I
want to do is jam this pen inside my skull. Last time I went to the
bathroom I gouged the fuck out of my ear and then tried to wash
the blood away. Judging by the way the woman is scowling at me,
I'm bleeding again. Shit—you know what, I get it. I figured out the
code. The woman is doing "The Itsy Bitsy Spider" song. She's turn-
ing her hands into a spider. Didn't I used to sing it to you? Hard to
think it through.

. . . I may have done something bad. I don't know how much
time has passed since my last entry. I dozed off. When an attendant
shook me awake to ask if I needed medical attention, I snapped. He
surprised me, and I shoved him. He slunk away. I think maybe he's
getting reinforcements and notifying the authorities. The woman
and kid are gone. In fact, I'm the only person left in the car. I turned
to this journal because I have nowhere else to go. I was hoping that
writing might help. Concentrate on one word at a time. One word
and then another word and another word and another word and
another word and another word and another word. How many
words do I need until I'm home with you? One word, two word,
three word, four word, five word, back word, for word, up word,

down word . . . I can't. They're coming for me. I know it. I need to get out of here.

Speck flips through the rest of the blank pages to make sure he isn't missing anything. It ends so abruptly. He returns to the beginning and searches for clues. Then he is startled by the man sitting in the chair across from him. It's as if Nolan suddenly materialized. The boy wonders how long he's been there.

"Bathroom's free, Mr. Petro." Nolan is leaning forward with his elbows on his knees, staring through red-veined eyes.

The boy has forgotten that he needs to pee. "It's Speck," he says, setting the journal aside.

"You finished."

"Yes."

"Was it about love?"

"No. It's about a soldier who loses his shit."

"'Loses his shit'?"

"His words. You have an ear ache?" Speck points a finger at the cotton ball crammed in Nolan's ear.

"It's nothing." Nolan sits upright and cracks his neck. It's hard to sit still.

"Bill Gent had an ear ache."

"It happens."

"Gus had one, too."

Nolan leans forward again. "Listen, Mr. Petro . . ."

"Speck."

"Right. Speck. We should talk about what happened last night."

"I know what happened. Wasps crawled into his head, he lost his shit, and he shot himself."

Nolan wonders if he heard the boy correctly. "What?"

"Nothing."

"You said something. That's for sure." Nolan feels his patience waning. He can't handle his ex-wife's weird kid right now. "Look," he says as he uses the arms of the chair to stand. "There's a lot to do. People need me right now. I'm not feeling my best, but that doesn't matter. Sometimes we just have to push through. I'm asking for your cooperation."

"All right. What can I do?"

"First of all, call your mother and explain what happened. Actually, scratch that. Let your brother call." Nolan makes his way into the kitchen and finds a napkin. He dabs the blood away.

"She won't be able to answer."

"He can leave a message."

"Should I wake him up?"

"Yeah," Nolan says, and then changes his mind. "No, forget it. Let him sleep. I've got to get to the hospital."

"Can I come?" the boy says, hopping out of his seat. He puts the journal back in the butterfly box. Here, he sees, is his opportunity.

Nolan squints. It helps temporarily ease the pain in his head. "Why?"

"I just stood there last night and didn't do anything when Ms. Muller carried Gus off. I should have helped."

"She was in shock. There was nothing you could do."

"Still. I was the last one to see Gus alive. Maybe that means something?"

Nolan grimaces. "Only one way to find out. Use the bathroom first." Nolan replaces the cotton swab with an extra one he has shoved into his pocket. "And, Speck?"

"Yeah?"

"Don't say anything stupid."

18.

Madison wakes up because there's something crawling across her wrist. She bolts upright and slaps at her tattoo.

"Ouch," Clara responds snaking her hand away.

"Mom?" Madison uncoils from the cramped position in the hospital chair where she had been watching over her mother. The doctor insisted on keeping Clara overnight since her heart rate was accelerated.

"Fifi."

"Yeah," Madison replies. Her mouth is dry. She does her best to pull herself together. "I was going to show you."

"It's lovely." Clara reclines against a wall of pillows, alert. The doctor checked on her earlier. She's been cleared to go. "Mom would like it."

"I'm glad you think so. It's how I remember her. Fierce and confident."

"Just like you."

"Like you, too, Mom."

"Wrong," Clara's voice breaks, and her eyes flash as she says this. "I'm like Dad. That sneaky old fool. He'd follow Mom to hell. Chased her there, too. He fed off her strength."

"Mom . . ."

"Don't interrupt," Clara's voice turns icy. "That's what love is, Maddy. Learn from it. Don't go rescuing a man unless you're willing to let him drag you down."

"All right." Madison brushes her hair away from her face. As she does so she momentarily misses the familiarity of the bracelets.

Clara stretches and places a hand on her daughter's knee. The day is bright outside. "I was watching you sleep. Such troubled dreams."

"I'm all right."

"You should leave, Madison. I'm told there are nice places in this world."

"It's nice here with you."

"Don't be in such a hurry to stay."

"I don't have anywhere else to go," Madison says softly.

"That's my fault. I've been selfish with you."

"We have the business to run. Now that I'm out of school, I can take on more responsibilities."

"No. That's a mistake I won't let you make."

Madison can't control a flash of heat rising to her face. She stands and turns her emotions away from Clara. "I'm the mistake, Mom. I wish you would admit it."

Clara slides out of the bed. She approaches Madison from behind and wraps her arms around her. She can feel how rigid her daughter's body is. "Fine," she whispers. "I admit it. You win. How can I make it up to you?"

Madison doesn't bother battling back the tears, and she doesn't try to break out of the embrace.

The weight of someone on top of him awakens Hudson. For a split-second he thinks it might be Madison.

"Say, Sleepyhead?" Crowley hisses. He pins Hudson's arms tightly behind his knees and uses his hands to hold the young man down in bed. "If there's anything that I've learned this morning it's that a person should lock his doors if he doesn't want intruders busting up his walls. Ruining his hard work." Crowley slaps Hudson lightly across the cheek.

Hudson struggles. He tries to make sense of the situation. He wonders where his brother and father are, if he's alone in the house, if he should cry out. "Look, I got a little drunk last night . . ."

Crowley wraps a dirty hand across Hudson's mouth. "What kind of punishment do you deserve?"

Hudson's scream for help is muffled.

"Nobody's here. Nobody cares." Crowley removes his hand and tightens his hold on Hudson's neck. "When I was a boy and misbehaved, I got a spanking. Your daddy ever give you one of those?"

The young man forces his body to relax. There's no use in struggling. He stares at the cleft in Crowley's chin and keeps his mouth shut.

"I'm sure old Nolan won't mind if I give you a good whack. Roll over, son."

Without much effort, Crowley tosses the sheets aside and flips Hudson over in the bed. The man's body has been hardened into steel from the job. He crams Hudson's head into the pillow and squeezes the young man like an accordion so that his ass is sticking out and exposed.

"Please," Hudson pleads out of the corner of his crushed mouth. "I'll give them back."

By swinging his hand wide Crowley is able to hit Hudson with great force. "One," he shouts. Then he repeats. "Two. Three."

Hudson tries to keep the tears from pinching out of his eyes as he bites the pillow.

"How many of my animals did you take? Four. Five. Six."

Hudson's head knocks against the headboard as he slides forward. His body contorts as he attempts to wiggle away from the pain.

"Let's have a look now," Crowley says unpeeling Hudson's shorts. "Oh yeah, that's going to leave a mark."

Hudson begins to drift away. He imagines himself elsewhere. Transported to the yard in the new house with the strong trees in the soft hammock on an afternoon . . .

"You seem to be enjoying this. Since your pants are down I may as well help myself to some." Crowley fumbles with his belt buckle.

. . . back inside the house he hears Madison call. She wants to know if he'd like a glass of . . . "No," Hudson shouts, resisting the urge to slip away. As Crowley pulls his belt through the loops of his pants Hudson channels his adrenaline and pushes up from the bed. Crowley loses his balance, momentarily, and as Hudson scrambles to get away, the man grab's his flailing legs.

"Oh, we're just getting started here, Beanpole."

Half off the bed, Hudson claws desperately for anything. His backpack is within reach. Inside is the hammer. Without hesitating the young man swings it around in a short arc and catches the crown of Crowley's head in a glancing blow. Crowley releases Hudson's legs and puts his hands to his head. He reclines in bed with a quizzical expression.

Hudson drops the hammer. He slips the backpack over his shoulder and scrambles away.

Outside, the sun is high, and it is hot. Crowley's van is nowhere in sight.

It's concealed behind some bushes along the side of the road. Hudson does not know where to go now. In a panic, he moves toward the fields.

Crowley brings his hands down in a cup from his head and stares at the little pool of blood. With a grunt, he stands, snatches the discarded hammer, and stumbles out of the house. His belt buckle rattles at his waist.

Eyes darting, searching for a place to hide, Hudson nearly steps on the circular wooden top covering up the entrance to the bomb shelter. In a flash, the young man drops to his knees and throws his back into sliding the cover free.

Crowley is momentarily blinded by the sun. He trips down the porch steps. Shading his eyes with the hammer, he squints at the horizon and sees the boy down by the field.

With his hands fumbling, it is difficult for Hudson to slide the lid away. Although he has tugged his shorts back up he feels the urge to reach back and pull them higher. When the opening is clear, he turns in time to see Crowley barreling down with the hammer poised. On instinct, Hudson rolls out of the way. The man plows full-steam forward and topples into the hole.

Hudson bolts down the pathway and into the forest.

Crowley hits the bottom with a thud. The hammer clatters into the dark. He isn't sure how he suddenly got here. One moment he was in pursuit of the boy, the next he is splayed out at the bottom of a well with a circle of light overhead. He tries to get his bearings by sitting upright. There's a ladder in front of him that leads out. To his side the tunnel continues. His ankle, he finds as he uses the ladder to stand, is broken or else badly twisted. It's a kind of pain he can ignore.

Scanning the concrete floor for the hammer, Crowley hears a low buzzing sound like a distant lullaby. Sometimes, when he was a boy, he'd hear his mom in the next room humming Gabriel softly to sleep. Crowley's thin lips are curling into a smile when the wasps attack.

Hudson has sprinted nearly to the railroad tracks before he remembers that he is without shoes. His bare feet have been tenderized.

Tossing a quick glance behind him, something he has been doing compulsively, Hudson drops to the ground and removes the semi-dry shoes from his backpack. The woods are quiet again, and when he begins heaving in low, dry, hacking sobs, the pain-filled agony echoes against the tree limbs. With his head bent, he cannot see that he is crouching beneath one of the many nests that wasps have formed in the forest. The insects have either killed or scared off any animal within a square mile—from the edge of the Summerfield subdivision all the way back to the Muller vineyard—and in squadrons spreading from the epicenter in the blind Speck discovered days ago, the wasps are taking over.

The glass animals in the open backpack wink at Hudson. "You are so ugly," he whispers.

With a grunt, Hudson rises to his feet and begins the familiar trek along the railroad—*five thousand, three hundred and eleven ties to go.*

19.

Nolan buys flowers in the lobby of the hospital before heading to the room, Speck trailing quietly behind. The boy hasn't said a word about all the swerving in the pickup on the way here nor is he going to mention anything about the sway in Nolan's strides.

Madison and Clara are both sitting on the bed laughing when the two enter.

"Knock, knock," Nolan says. "Are we interrupting?"

Clara hops off the bed. "No, of course not. We were just getting ready to leave. Those lilacs are lovely, thank you." Clara takes the bouquet from Nolan and kisses him affectionately on the mouth. "You must see the beautiful tattoo that Maddy has gotten." Taking his hand, Clara leads Nolan to the bed.

"It's nothing, really," Madison says, running a hand through the tangles in her hair. Despite her reluctance, she exposes her wrist for Nolan to see.

When he takes his hand away from Clara's Nolan notices that it is trembling. "It's nice," he says, burying his hands in his pockets.

"Can I see?" Speck says, hurrying over.

"I'm thinking of getting something done, too," Clara says. "What do you think?"

"It's a great idea," Nolan agrees.

"Cool," Speck says to Madison. "What does it mean?"

"It doesn't have to mean anything," Nolan says. "Don't pry."

"She's like a guardian angel," Madison answers.

Seizing the opportunity—better now than never—Speck withdraws the note from his pocket and holds it out to Clara. "I found this," he says quickly, "on the stairs last night after you . . . it fell out of his pocket . . . it might not mean anything. I don't know why he misspelled the word."

"What are you talking about?" Nolan takes a step towards the boy, his hand outstretched. "I thought we agreed you weren't going to be dumb."

Speck tucks the note under his arm and cowers.

"It's all right," Clara says. She puts her hand on Nolan's bicep and bends down to look Speck in the eyes. "Speck, could you show me what you've got there?"

"I never meant to keep it a secret. Here," the boy thrusts the piece of paper into Clara's hands, "it doesn't even make sense."

Clara stands upright and reads the note. She reads it again. Then she nods her head as if agreeing to some question she's been asked.

"What's it say?" Madison asks.

"*Raze the fields.*"

"Only he misspelled *raise,*" Speck offers.

Clara smiles, despite herself. The note is something, after all, and she has Speck to thank for giving it to her. "When you spell the word the way my father did it means 'burn to the ground.' He wants us start over. And that's exactly what we'll do. After we have a little party."

"Mom and I have come up with a plan," Madison says. "We'll have the services at the Episcopal Church on Grove and then invite the community to the house for a reception."

"Are you sure you're up for that?" Nolan says, facing Clara.

"Yes, yes," she says. "Everyone will gossip no matter what we do. I'd rather they do it to my face. But I want to be quick about it."

"If I hear an unkind word about your father . . ." Nolan steadies himself against the side of the bed.

"I'll keep you by my side. We'll get everyone nice and drunk."

"Don't uncork the reserve," Nolan mutters.

Surprised at the turn of events, Speck relaxes. He wasn't sure how Clara would respond. It couldn't have gone better. He asks, "What can I do?"

"You, my darling boy," Clara says, "will be in charge of my father's most prized possession."

Hudson hears a train and slips into the scruff. Instead of looking away, he tries to meet the gazes of the blurry passengers peering out at his disheveled character. He raises his hand and waves. "Hello," he shouts, "you lucky fucks. Bye-bye, bye-bye."

After it is gone, Hudson hurries along. It has occurred to him that Crowley might drive back to his trailer once he has climbed out of the bomb shelter. Hudson is not sure how he will defend himself if the bastard does show up. The idea is to get in and out without being seen.

Hudson has had time to worry about what Crowley might do. The man could call the police. After all, he did break Crowley's taillight, bust up the new construction, and whack him in the head with a hammer. Right now, in fact, he is carrying a bagful of glass animals that belong to his mother. So, as the young man cautiously approaches the doublewide trailer, he half expects to see a police car and half expects to see Crowley's hideous van.

What Hudson doesn't expect to see as he creeps around the side of the trailer and turns to hurry up the wheelchair ramp where he can situate the figurines along the *Welcome* mat, knock on the door, and run, is Ms. Crowley perched in her chair on the stoop.

"Oh," Hudson says, freezing.

Ms. Crowley tilts her head around and widens her eyes in surprise. She maintains her composure, keeping her hands folded neatly in her lap, and says, "Oh. I have a visitor? You're that nice young man, my son."

Hudson battles back his instinct to flee. "I work with your son. You remember me?"

"I've got a head for faces. I don't get a lot of callers."

The simple clarity in Ms. Crowley's voice allows Hudson to relax. Letting up on the tension drains away his energy. He puts all his weight against the porch railing and sets the backpack on the wooden slats.

"Hot," Ms. Crowley states. "I thought the rain would help, but it didn't."

"Yes," Hudson replies. "I mean, no."

"Are you all right?"

Hudson runs his tongue over his busted lip. It has cracked again and tastes like loose change. "I didn't expect to see you."

"Let me get you some water," Ms. Crowley says, pushing herself up in her seat.

"I don't know."

"Has James done something bad again?" Ms. Crowley winces when her damaged foot touches the ground.

"What do you mean, again?"

The old woman exaggerates the pinch of pain she feels in her foot from yesterday's wound. There are parts of her body that feel much worse. She raises her leg so the raw-red cut is exposed in the wrinkled waves of her pruned foot.

Hudson takes the bait. "What happened?"

"Oh, nothing," she says, folding her age-spotted arms across her wide lap.

"Someone should look at that."

"Like who?" Ms. Crowley accidentally screeches. She scratches the bottom of her foot against the edge of the wheelchair so that it begins to bleed.

"A doctor. Your son. Stop doing that. You're making it worse."

"It itches."

"I'll call someone," Hudson says although, he realizes, he left his phone back home.

"Don't. If people come they'll take me away. If I go away I won't come back. Here isn't great, but it beats the alternative. I do have peroxide in my medicine cabinet." Ms. Crowley nods her head in the direction of the trailer and raises her painted-on eyebrows like two jittery gulls.

No way is Hudson going back in there. *But, still, wait*, he reconsiders, *maybe*. Hoisting the backpack, he says, "Wait here," before heading inside.

The moment he is inside Ms. Crowley climbs out of her chair and hobbles after him. "I'll get you a cup of water," she insists, closing the front door behind her.

Hudson is caught between Crowley's side of the apartment and the old woman's side. "I can get it myself."

"No, no," she shakes her head. "Fetch the medicine. It's behind the mirror. My door isn't locked."

Hudson tries to swallow down the heavily perfumed air. "All right."

"All right," Ms. Crowley parrots. "I do like callers, you know." When she sets her injured foot down on the worn carpet floor she leaves a bloodstain. "I'll whip up a sandwich, too. I make very good sandwiches. A boy like you should eat more."

With her back turned and in the kitchen, Hudson sprints into her apartment, hurries into the bedroom, opens the hutch doors, and situates the glass animals back on the shelves with the others. Then he scuttles to the bathroom. He rummages through the drawers behind the mirror—

taking too much time—and finally discovers a withered, crusty tube of ointment and a Band-Aid. As he lunges to the door he finds Ms. Crowley barring the exit.

"I forgot to ask, dear, do you like bologna or pimento loaf?"

"I'm not hungry."

"You're as thin as a rain drop."

"No, I'm not."

"Have a seat on my couch. I'll bring it to you."

Hudson tries to decide how he's going to get past her without doing more damage. "Ms. Crowley, I really need to . . ."

"Call me Sweetie Pie. My sons do."

"Yeah, well."

"What happened to your face? Let me have a look at it." The old woman closes the door. "That James is so wicked. You've got to be firm with him, Gabe. Fight back, for Christ's sake!"

Hudson tucks his lip into his mouth. He takes a quick step backwards. Through the bars in the window the sun cascades. Tiny dust particles float in an unsuspecting universe around the dowdy couch. "How about that glass of water?"

"I can see what he sees in you. If only you'd let me put my hand on your cheek for a moment. We help each other out, see?" Ms. Crowley steps forward, teetering on her damaged foot.

Hudson seizes the opportunity to dodge past her and to the door. As he struggles with the handle—she has locked them in—Ms. Crowley regains her balance and throws her arms around Hudson's shoulders.

"He'll hurt you again," she gasps, clawing.

Hudson pries the door open and attempts to spin out. She clings to the backpack, her mouth open in a vacant oval, moaning. He does his best to brace the old woman as she topples to the floor between the two sides of the trailer. "I'm sorry," he says. "I just wanted to return your animals. Your son keeps taking them."

Ms. Crowley's face is smashed flat against the floor. She contorts her body—bending her brittle spine—and flails. Before he can escape, Hudson hears her exclaim, "I know you are dead. I forgive you. Come back."

Back home Nolan sits at the kitchen counter with a phone book, a bottle of aspirin, and a cigarette. Ordinarily he smokes outside.

After they returned, he instructed Speck to try and find Hudson who had carelessly left the front door of the pink house wide open. Then Nolan began the difficult task of making calls. Because his hearing is shot in his right ear, he has to hold the phone awkwardly to his left ear while punching the numbers on the peach-colored and rarely used home phone. He battles the frequent waves of pain in his head. Nolan is the kind of man who believes he can convince himself, if he tries hard enough, that nothing's wrong. He has gotten by on headstrong denial his whole life. The sympathetic listeners on the other end mistake the strain and agony in his voice for grief.

Speck wanders towards the woods in search of his brother. Pepper tags along. As they pass, the boy glances into the hangar to make sure it's empty. All the dust that was kicked around last night has settled. The airplane looks exactly like it did the first time he saw it.

When Hudson emerges from the woods Pepper barks and sprints ahead to greet him. Speck stays put and waits for his brother. When he's close, the boy says, "You spend too much time in those woods."

Hudson's face is flushed. He'd like nothing more than to avoid the woods forever. "You see anyone strange around here?"

Speck nods his head. "We just got back."

Hudson continues past his brother on his way to the bomb shelter. The humid air is pungent with the sweet grape scent. "Have you noticed that all the rose bushes have died?" the boy says, trying to keep up.

A familiar feeling of dread paces Hudson as he approaches the hole. He doesn't know that Speck has asked him a question. Crowley could still be down there, unconscious from the fall. Or, he could be waiting to pull the young man down and finish what he started this morning. While he does not want to see what is below Hudson knows he must face it. If there's any danger here it's his job to shield his brother from it.

At the opening Hudson closes his eyes, says a quick prayer, takes a gulp of air, and peers down. Sunlight descends a few rungs on the ladder and then stops. Fishing through his backpack Hudson removes the flashlight, his heart thumping, and casts the light in. The concrete below is illuminated. There are no signs of Crowley. Hudson's hollow "Hello?" reports back unanswered. A single dead, up-turned wasp lies in repose in the halo of light.

"Is he down there?" Speck asks, sidling up to Hudson.

Hudson clicks the flashlight off and whirls on his brother. "Who? Why would he be? I thought you didn't see anyone?"

"The raccoon, Hud," Speck holds his hands out defensively. "Is it gone?"

"Right. Yeah. I think." Hudson tosses the backpack to the ground. "Help me slide this back.

Speck pushes while Hudson pulls, and they seal the shelter.

"You know," Speck says, wiping his hands on his shirt. "I have so many questions for you."

"I know, I'm sorry . . ."

"But I'm not going to ask you any of them."

"I appreciate . . ."

"Instead," Speck continues, "I'm going to go up to the house and help Ms. Muller with the funeral party. It's tomorrow, in case you don't know."

"I didn't. Thanks."

"It seems strange to me, to have a party. But I guess it makes sense. We have them on our birthday, why not on our deathday?"

"That does make . . ."

"I also cleaned up the room. What happened . . . , no, I'm not going to ask what happened. I don't appreciate you knocking my stuff around. My computer was on the floor."

"Was it broken?"

"No. And you don't get to ask questions."

"I'm sorry."

"I finally got a hold of Mom. She's on her way. She was worried, of course, and wanted to talk to you. I told her you were helping your Dad. You don't have to thank me."

"Thank you."

"Don't. Now unless you have to run off again, I could use some help. We have work to do."

"All right, Boss," Hudson says. When he bends down to retrieve his backpack he can't help remembering this morning. He tugs at his shorts. Hudson would like to tell his brother about Crowley, to warn him, if nothing else. At the same time, he can't beat back the rising shame that blooms when he recollects. The bastard is probably licking his wounds over at Moonshadows or else back at his trailer trying to explain himself to his mother. Hudson's own mother will be here soon, and that's a comfort. With a little luck he can keep the incident a secret. Just move on. One thing he won't do is let his brother out of his sight. "What did you have in mind?"

Speck turns his back and strides towards the hanger. "Let's go fetch the *Widowmaker.*"

20.

*In order to protect their offspring from Muscidifurax raptor, it's been
discovered that fruit flies will lay their eggs in droplets of alcohol
that develop from fermenting apples or grapes. Once hatched, the
fly larvae will soak up the alcohol like sponge cake. When the tiny
wasp parasite attempts to incubate the fly larvae, it will become too
inebriated to lay the clutch of eggs. The buzzed wasp will topple over
or else bumble around in erratic elliptical flight patterns which often
attract observant sparrows.*

In the rented limo on their way back to the vineyard for the reception
Speck reflects on the ceremony. Since this is his first funeral he didn't
know what to expect. This morning, when he woke up, his arms were in
pain. Yesterday evening he and Hudson scrubbed the B-26 Martin Marauder clean. They wheeled it out of the hanger and into a patch of grass,
and then waxed it. On display, the plane looks as good as new. Speck
wanted it to resemble the way that it might have looked to Gus when the
old man was young. The soreness in his arms has diminished as the day
develops.

At the church in his rented suit Speck didn't expect Gus to be there in
the closed coffin. There were many mourners; the pews were crowded.
People filed up to the front and had a private moment with the old man
before offering condolences to Clara and Madison who stood somber
near the exit. When Nolan approached, Speck noticed, he took a knee
and set his head against the cool cherry wood where he left it for several

minutes. Speck wondered if he had fallen asleep. Eventually a member of the Veterans of Foreign Wars lightly tapped Nolan on the arm and, with difficulty, he walked away.

From Hudson Speck learned that the coffin had been rented, too. The next stop for Gus was the crematory. Then he'd be mixed with Elizabeth and scattered in the dirt after the field was burned to the ground. Then the two of them would be in the wine, somehow. That's the idea, anyway, as Speck understands it.

Now, as they pull into the estate, the boy wonders what wine tastes like. Stepping out of the cool air-conditioned limo and into the stifling heat, he fiddles with his clip-on tie.

The gift shop has been rearranged to accommodate mourners. The merchandise is in storage, and a spread of cheese, crackers, and bottles of *Muller Roux* have been uncorked and are breathing on the tasting tables. On the walls Clara has mounted pictures of Gus that she dug up from her old photo albums and a framed newspaper clipping written about the couple—the war veterans turned vintners—from several years ago.

Down the slope in the lawn is a tent with more tables, food, and *Icicle Rouge*. Clara wanted to offer her guests something cool in order to battle back the heat. Hudson volunteered to be the bartender. He will serve the drinks and replenish the ice so the bottles stay cold.

Arranged on easels in a semi-circle around the Marauder are Gus's paintings of plane parts. Few people knew of the old man's hobby, and even if they are not impressed by what they see, they can appreciate how he tried to stay busy without Elizabeth. If onlookers expect to find some clue as to why Gus killed himself brushed into the art—subconscious warning signs—they are disappointed. That doesn't quell the speculations, however. The ruddy shadow extending across the cockpit could be seen as a gloved finger of death. Don't those propeller blades seem razor-blade sharp, sharper than necessary? Is that a tiny noose curled around the landing gear? In a way, if you tilt your head just so, the wings are shaped like bullets.

Just to be on the safe side, before situating himself at the tent Hudson did a quick survey of the property in search of Crowley. He didn't find anyone. Now that the crowd has gathered he's pretty confident that Crowley will stay away.

Hudson wants to repair the fracture in his relationship with Madison.

The two have barely spoken since the other night, and every time he tries to catch her eyes, Madison quickly looks away. When he attempted to approach, she has backed off. All he has been able to do is stand in line and offer his condolences like all the other grievers.

Hudson also knows he has work to do with his father. They haven't broached the topic of the slap. The fact that the son raised his hand against the father. When Hudson made a half-hearted attempt this morning—"Hey, Dad, I'm sorry about the other day . . ."—Nolan had waved him off. "Don't worry about it," he said, avoiding eye contact.

Now, Nolan looks like hell back at the main house. Hudson suspects his old man has been hitting the bottle hard. His eyes are bloodshot, his words, when he infrequently speaks, are slurred, and he can't seem to put one straight foot in front of the other. Hudson's happy he's down here staying busy pouring ice wine to a steady line of thirsty mourners.

When people start arriving Madison stays at her mother's elbow where she has been all day. Earlier, when Hudson tried to console her and whisper, "I'm sorry," she folded her arms and turned away. The last thing she needs right now is relationship drama. The fury that she felt back at the unfinished house when she stormed away (and he didn't chase after her) quickly morphed into shock when she discovered what her grandfather had done. Before she could process what had happened she recognized the delicate state of her mother and has been sentinel by her side ever since. Surprisingly, her mother is all right. The instinctive gesture of dragging Gus to the airplane in the barn where Elizabeth took her own life may have somehow given Clara solace. The cordial and composed person speaking calmly with well-wishers right now seems authentic. Her mother being all right makes it easier for Madison to grapple with her own grief. She chastises herself for thinking about Hudson now— she can see him under the tent and notices that Aubrey and a few other townies are loitering—instead of remembering her grandfather. She pinches the inside of her arm with her fingernails and orders herself not to care.

Nolan leans on the front porch unsteadily. When the unbearable roll of pain crests he clutches the rail and digs his fingernails into the wood. He fights to stay in the moment. For Clara. For Gus. When anyone approaches him to offer their sympathies he says, "Gus was the best man I've ever known." Three concerned V.F.W. members amble over to Nolan and ask if he's all right. Unable to hear, he misreads them and says, "Gus was the best man I've ever known. I will really miss him."

Once the men are gone Nolan feels Speck tugging at his jacket sleeve.

"What should I do?" the boy asks.

"Stay out of the way," Nolan murmurs.

"Can I take off this suit?"

"What?" Nolan tries to focus his attention. "No. I don't know. Don't get it dirty. I'm paying for it. You think your mother will reimburse me? Or your father, Mr. Petro?"

Speck backs off. He can sense the head of steam building and doesn't want any part of it. He meanders through the crowd down to his brother. Hudson is busy pouring wine. The wine looks like Sprite. Speck wonders what would happen if he just grabs one of the open bottles and casually walks away. Will anyone say anything? Not yet. Five paces. Nothing. Ten. Fifteen. Not a word. Soon, he's sliding into the privacy of the barn.

Without the airplane, the hangar feels enormous. Speck sits on Gus's bench next to several canisters of blue paint. He holds the bottle up into the light. The Muller insignia—an M overtop a W—looks the same upside down. He takes a small sip and holds it in his mouth. It feels like a million stinging chiggers fighting to get out. Swallowing is difficult. The boy battles back a gag. "*Icicle Rouge*," he says. "It does taste like shit." He tries it again. This time he does not bother to let it linger. While it burns going down, it's not intolerable. He wonders how much he'll need to consume in order to feel something. Who can say how long it takes for alcohol to affect the alchemy of an inquisitive child's brain?

Later, when he hears a voice—*Hey there, Kiddo, take it easy*—he's caught off guard. He spins around, losing his balance and toppling to the floor, searching for the source. Though his vision is blurry—his eyes are playing tricks—he can see someone peering down from the loft. It looks like someone, anyway. A man, with red hair, he thinks. Or it might just be a stack of boxes gathering light from the setting sun.

"Hello?" the boy says, his tentative voice echoing. "Is someone there?"

"Look who it is," Bowlie says to Hudson when he is at the front of the line, "Nobody."

"What?" Hudson says. He's not sure what the chubby kid in the too-small jacket is talking about. With his head down and doing his job he has lost track of time.

"Nobody doesn't remember us, Bowlie," Pike says. "You drink my beer, ignore our invitation to our party, break Aubrey's poor little heart, and then pretend we don't exist. Well, I've got news for you," Pike gathers a half-dozen plastic cups full of the ice wine, "when you're gone, nobody will even remember you were here. You're a fart in the wind."

Laughing, Bowlie intentionally knocks over one of the cups. The two make farting noises with their mouths and carry their drinks toward the plane.

The young woman with short blond hair sidesteps the pooling wine dripping onto the ground. "Someone spilled," she says tersely. "People can be so rude, don't you think?"

Hudson remembers her from the pond. It's Audrey or Aubrey or something. He realizes that he is out of paper towels.

"It's Aubrey, in case you forgot."

Hudson notices that she has painted her nails black. Perhaps for this occasion. "I remember," he says.

"Having a good vacation?" Aubrey frowns in her heavily applied red lipstick.

Hudson lets his shoulders sag. "It's not what I expected," he says quietly.

"Can't say any of this surprises me. Just fill my cup to the brim so I don't have to keep returning."

"I need to get paper towels," Hudson says.

Ignoring this, Aubrey hisses, "I told you it's hereditary."

"Maybe," Hudson replies, distractedly. He spies his little brother stumbling out of the barn and toward the pink house. "But I don't think so."

"How else do you explain it?"

"I can't," he says.

Mourners behind Aubrey fidget impatiently. It's easier to sympathize with a good buzz going. A curious wasp leaves one of the many nests in the vineyard and buzzes over to the tent. It curlicues above the people enticed by the sweet wine.

The man scrambles down the ladder from the loft like a monkey and is, in the long blink of an eye, standing before the boy.

"You real?" Speck asks.

I'm Tolly, the man says. *You can call me Real if you'd like.*

"You're from the book?"

What book?

"Bill's book."

Have you seen him?

"Not him, no. Book's in the butterfly box."

That's a tongue twister.

"Book's in the butterfly box, book's in the butterfly box, book's in the butterfly box . . ."

I'm glad that you found me.

"You found me."

Tolly shrugs his shoulders. *Same difference.*

"Hey, do you want to hear something funny?" the boy asks. He takes another gulp from the bottle and finds that it's almost empty.

Sure.

"Well, my real name is Joshua, and Josh is short for Joshua which is a joke which is why I don't go by it and everyone calls me Speck—except for Mr. Bastard—and you'll never guess what I discovered about waps. . . ."

Wasps.

" . . . wasps. Fear of wasps."

Spheksophobia.

"Ha! Yes. Right. Just like me."

You and me both, Kiddo.

"Anyway. That's funny to me. I do hate those fuckers." The boy tilts back the bottle and drains it. Tolly has to grab ahold of Speck's shoulder to keep him from falling again. "Anyway, anyway," the boy says. "That wasn't bad. But I better focus. I know why you're here."

You do.

"To find your friend."

Gent.

"He's real, too. Or was."

I'm here to find out.

"Let's go get his journal."

Book's in the butterfly box.

"If you'll excuse me," Hudson says looking around Aubrey to the people in line. "I've got to get some paper towels. Feel free to help yourselves," he states slamming the bottle down hard on the table and splashing some of the spilled wine on Aubrey's dress.

"You're an asshole," Aubrey says.

Hudson strides purposefully to the pink house. As he rounds the corner he sees his brother slumped over on the porch muttering to himself.

"Speck?" Hudson says, hurrying over. "What happened to you?"

"You got the book?" the boy says.

"All right," Hudson says, hoisting his brother up by the elbows and pulling him inside the house. "Let's get you cleaned up."

In his haste to take care of his brother Hudson does not notice that the hatch to the trap door in the den has been busted off its hinges.

"I found it in the woods. By the tracks. Near the telephone pole with my name."

"How much did you drink?" Hudson asks.

"Watch out for the poison ivy."

"You're a mess, kid," Hudson says. He struggles into the bathroom and tries to maneuver the boy out of his clothes.

"Your Dad's not going to be happy about the suit. I might have slipped in the dirt."

Back on the porch Nolan continues to grip the woman's hand—offered sympathetically—long after he is supposed to let go. "He was the best man I've ever known," Nolan says loudly. He's pretty sure he'll collapse if he lets go.

"You're hurting me," the woman hisses. "Let go."

"What did you say?" Nolan releases the woman. Her husband, a man who owns a Subaru dealership, breaks away from his conversation to check on her.

Madison senses the mounting tension. She leaves her mother's side.

"I think I'm going to need ice," the woman says to her husband.

"You don't think I'm nice?" Nolan says. "Well you're not so fucking great either."

"Wow," Madison swoops in. "All right," she says, grabbing Nolan's arm and guiding him to the swing at the other end of the porch. "Let's just sit down and relax a while, shall we?"

Nolan stumbles toward the swing and then shakes Madison's arm away. "Don't placate me," he shouts.

"Do not raise your voice." Madison narrows her eyes. With a quick shove, she pushes Nolan onto the swing. "We do not need a scene. Just sit there and sober up."

Nolan, hot now, clenches his fist and struggles to find his feet. Without his balance, he slips to one knee. "Who do you think you are?" he asks.

Madison turns on her heels and strides away.

With effort, Nolan manages to climb back onto the swing. He throws his legs over the side, cramped in his rented suit, and sets his throbbing head against the arm of the swing. He grinds his teeth as another bout of pain flashes through his skull. The hungry wasp larvae have emerged from the acid sac and are ferociously gnashing. They'll gorge and then rest. In a moment, the wave will subside and Nolan's exhausted body will shut down. He will not be out long. The noises in his head sound like macaroni being ladled into a dish. The only thing the man can think to do is get up. He staggers down the porch steps and collapses in the gravel, holding his head. By now, most of the mourners have been giving him a wide berth. Those that see him stumble let him be.

Nolan tries to stay focused. His eyes fall onto Clara who is standing on the edge of the parking lot. Her face is pinched tight, and she is staring intently down at the field. Following her gaze like a lifeline Nolan peers past the sporadic mourners, around the tent, and finally to the airplane. Two young men have pried open the hatch and are clowning around inside the cockpit, yanking the steering wheel and handling the gears. Nolan can't understand why the adults are placidly standing by like idiots. Like this is some plastic coin-operated toy outside the mall meant to entertain children. Some fantastic game. They have no idea. This plane saved lives.

Madison, in conversation by the minister's Toyota, notices the rabid look in Nolan's eyes a moment too late.

Nolan snaps. All the pain coalesces into fury. He pitches himself head-long down the short hill, his funeral coat flapping as if trying to hold him back. Though he isn't aware, Nolan is emitting a feral growl as he charges. Most people have time to step aside. Pike and Bowlie also hear and then see the frenzied man heading in their direction. Cursing, they slide the cockpit door closed and fumble with the inside lock.

Nolan scratches up the wing and yanks at the handle. Blood spurts from his ear and trickles onto his collar. His eyes are veiny, and his lips are papery. When he can't manage the door Nolan pounds on the glass with his bare wrists, fully committed to his blind rage.

In World War II sometimes planes would go down in enemy territory. Martin Marauders were designed to withstand light, direct, foot-soldier attack so that the crew inside might have a chance to get their wits about them before braving the outside. Try as he might, Nolan is not getting in.

After a minute as the shock wears off the gathering crowd, Bowlie's father, and a few other men clamber onto the plane and attempt to restrain the madman. Nolan swings his clenched fists in wide arcs. Bowlie's dad sweeps a leg and Nolan spills to the ground. Even with the wind knocked out of him, Nolan keeps fighting. His flails give way to convulsions. He minces his tongue as he writhes.

21.

In China, the Asian Giant Hornet is responsible for killing over forty people and injuring more than 1,600. The toxic sting from the insect can cause anaphylactic shock and renal failure. Many victims have been stung well over two hundred time. One woman, who was recovering in the hospital, told doctors that the hornets chased her for nearly a mile. "The more you run, the more they want to chase you," she said.

Recently, the Asian Giant Hornet was discovered in Arlington Heights, Illinois by a man playing baseball with his son in the late afternoon. When he bent down to retrieve an errant ball that had rolled under a hibiscus, he was attacked—stung in the neck and face. His son ran over and squashed the insect with his mitt. Because he was having difficulty breathing, the man went to the hospital, and, thinking it might be of use, the boy brought the dead hornet cupped inside his glove. It's easy to mistake the Asian Giant Hornet with the Cicada Killer—they are both as long as a human thumb and have similar markings. One distinction, however, are the yellow-orange and brownish-black bands on its body which, in some ways, resemble a bee.

As a precaution, concerned citizens made flyers with pictures of Vespa mandarinia—the mass murderer—and plastered the town. Stores ran out of cans of Raid. The people of Arlington Heights developed itchy trigger fingers and spritzed anything that could fly including, in some circumstances, fireflies and ladybugs.

Inside the house, Hudson tends to his brother. He doesn't care that he's abandoned his post at the wine tent outside, and he's too preoccupied to hear all the commotion his father is making.

The first thing Hudson did is try to force Speck to throw up into the toilet. The boy hacked and coughed and complained and did not get much out. Then, he hauled Speck into the bathtub and cleaned him as best as he could. After the bath, Hudson slid his brother into pajamas and forced him to drink glass after glass of water. Now the boy is fitfully sleeping in bed. Hudson can see his brother's eyes moving rapidly beneath the lids. It didn't take him long to slip into a dream. The pained look on Speck's face is familiar to Hudson; it's the same look he saw back at home when his brother was battling back night terrors, shortly after witnessing the bicyclist who got swiped by the cab.

Next to the bed, on the nightstand, is Speck's radio. Hudson gently eases the headphones into his brother's ears and turns the classical music on low.

For a while, Hudson sits by his brother and runs his fingers gently through the recently cut red hair. He battles back the creeping memories of what took place in his own bed not long ago and resists the urge to wonder, again, where Crowley is. Instead, he tries to clear his mind. Think about something else like the book on the nightstand—*A Confederacy of Dunces*—that he hasn't even opened since arriving. He's not in the mood to read it right now. His brother is the one who has been reading this summer. Hudson surveys the room but can't seem to locate Speck's book.

The solider enters the woods, journal in hand. Tolly is following the boy's directions. He hurries down the dirt road. Nobody from the party sees him. A white dog scampers out of an old vehicle junkyard in pursuit. Stopping only to make sure that the animal is friendly, Tolly forges ahead.

Tolly doesn't have time to read the journal. It's getting too dark to see well. He does recognize the handwriting. It's something Bill wrote in all the time. And it's proof that Gent was here. He's one step closer to solving the mystery.

Once he arrived in New York City, Tolly escorted the monkey remains to his uncle at the Primate Lab. Together, they dissected Willy. The inside of the skull looked like a pumpkin that a kid tried to hollow out with a dull spoon. Scrutinizing further, they found a tiny wasp pupa embedded in the brain. At first, Tolly's uncle suspected that the wasp somehow got into the cooler after Willy was dead. Upon further investigation, and with Tolly's insistence that the makeshift tomb had been sealed tight, they started to make sense of the situation.

"You know the way, don't you, boy?" Tolly says to the dog. He easily cuts through the trampled trail—Hudson has been this way so many times before—and soon arrives at the railroad tracks.

Parasitologists discover new insects all the time. Just last year, scientists identified at least one hundred and seventy-seven distinct species of parasitic wasps. In order to support the uncle's hypothesis (that they had discovered a breed capable of entering the headspace of mammals and incubating in the brain), they needed live samples. And in order to do that, they needed to find William Gent.

Tolly walks along the railroad, behind the dog. Now that he's outside the forest he can hear how hushed the world is. He's too busy thinking about silence to notice the abandoned wasp nest under the railroad ties.

Andrea Davis, the woman who was on the train when the wasps buzzed into the windows and attacked, arrived in Niagara Falls expecting a rendezvous with her online lover. When he didn't show up, she flew into a rage, busted up the hotel room, and threw herself into the turbulent water. Tolly learned all this from authorities when he was trying to track down Gent. He knew Gent got on a train heading to Rochester. And he knew, having spoken to Gent's sister, that his friend had never made it home. Somewhere between Penn Station and Rochester, Gent had gotten off. Tolly uncovered the incident of the wasp attack from the Amtrak logs, spoke to all of the victims who complained about getting stung, and then tried to reach Andrea. From her husband, he learned about the suicide. In Buffalo he interviewed the hotel clerk and learned that Andrea acted like an angry drunk. The clerk had seen that kind of behavior before but was surprised how such a small woman could manufacture such explosive violence. From the coroner, who did not perform an autopsy, Tolly learned that Andrea's head must have smashed against the rocks because it was badly damaged.

The telephone poles are spaced about one hundred feet apart. Tolly inspects each one as he hurries along, searching for the boy's name. The evening somehow seems hotter in the quiet. Before long, Tolly finds a pole with the name—*Joshua*—etched neatly into the coarse wooden grain.

"This it, boy?"

The dog eases into the trees. He's impatient for the man to follow and see for himself what's already been discovered.

By contacting hospitals and pouring over obituaries Tolly learned about Gus's suicide. While there's nothing unusual about an old man taking his own life, the way he did it, by putting the pistol into his ear, encouraged Tolly to investigate. And this paid off. Here he is now, fending away branches, walking along the same path that his infected comrade blindly ran in an effort to escape the pain, pushing through spider webs spun from the same spiders that spooled out webs that Tolly now breaks through. He crashes past the tree line and into the clearing where the timid stream mumbles on its way to converge with other tributaries all destined to flow into the cold, deep water of Seneca Lake.

Tolly sees the white dog sitting beneath the oak tree patiently waiting with a bone in his mouth. And it's all a dream, what happens next, Tolly rushing over—*Give that to me, boy*—when the dog refuses and prances away, thinking this is some kind of game, and in some ways it is; the man chases the animal around and around in a small, tight circle, yipping excitedly and the sound awakens the sleepy wasps in the tree. They fall upon Tolly without fanfare.

Pepper drops the bone and bolts.

The man is stung repeatedly. The idea is to incapacitate him so that the queen can easily slip into his ear and deposit her brood. Tolly waves his arms around in an effort to ward the wasps away, which only enrages them further. He stumbles to the water and submerges himself. This shakes off several insects but not all of them. The venom from the stings increases his heart rate, and it's difficult for him to hold his breath and submerge— stay under water long enough so that they all just go away—so he surfaces, shakes his body vehemently and runs. Keeps his head down. Puts one foot in front of the other. Backtracks. Trips, turns an ankle, gets back up, falls, rises. With the wasps buzzing so close to his ears he can't hear a thing. It's only when he's nearly atop it that he realizes a slow moving CSX train hauling trash out of New York City is on the tracks and passing.

Without thinking, the soldier pitches himself into a mostly empty boxcar. He rolls feverishly in the refuse crushing the insidious insects.

Gent's diary slips from Tolly's grasp and gets lost in the trash heap. The man will drift in and out of consciousness—between an idea and reality—not much more than a figment of a fitful child's imagination. He'll be resurrected, years later when Speck becomes Joshua, through the hazy scaffolding of memory.

The platoon of wasps falls back. It's late, and they're too tired to chase machines.

22.

The Emerald Cockroach Wasp, also known as the Jewel Wasp, stings its victim the first time in order to disable the front legs. Cockroaches are much larger than Ampulex compressa, but they are not smarter. The second sting from the wasp is delivered into the roach's brain— the sub-esophageal ganglia—which does not kill the victim, rather, it switches off the instinct to flee. Like humans, cockroaches will either fight or run when posed with a threat, and the jewel wasp has figured out a way to circumvent that survival impulse. There is enough poison in the sting to keep the roach alive, zombified, and do the wasp's bidding. Using an antenna as a leash, the wasp will lead the victim into her underground lair and lay an egg on its abdomen. Then she'll leave. The cockroach will stay put. It is difficult to speculate what it might be thinking, awaiting certain doom. Cockroaches are disease-addled which wards most parasites away. After hatched, though, the larval wasps secrete antimicrobial droplets from their mouths which kill what would otherwise be deadly bacteria inside the roach's body. And into the body the larva burrows. Once inside, it can feast upon the innards, build a cocoon, and mature in the still-living host. What kind of pain must the roach feel? Researchers cannot be sure. In a little while, the adult emerald wasp will crawl out of the cocoon, gorge itself again, wiggle out of the body, scuttle up and out of the hole its mother made, spread its quivering wings, and fly off leaving the roach buried in an unmarked grave.

Microbiologists are fascinated by the miraculous Emerald Wasp as are neurochemists. The precision with which the wasp inserts its stinger—if it's a millimeter to the left or right it will kill its host—is something even the most steady-handed surgeon would envy. The brightest minds in the world are working tirelessly to figure out exactly how the toxins incapacitate the brain. Just think what a synthetic drug made from the wasp venom could do for modern medicine. For the wounded and weak. To combat disease. Compressed into a bomb.

If cockroaches had brains like humans and scientists were emerald wasps, just think how our species might evolve.

Speck rolls back and forth, dreaming of being blanketed by wasps, and if Hudson weren't there to steady him he'd fall off the bed.

"It's just a nightmare," Hudson whispers although he knows Speck cannot hear. It helps to say, to go through the motion, to participate in the belief that soothing words mean something. The borders of the window darken. Without his consent, Hudson sees his bed and comes dangerously close to remembering—*It's over. You got away*—the way his head smacked against the wall—*didn't even leave a bruise*—the sting of Crowley's flat hand against his ass—*the marks faded and are gone*—the rattle of the belt buckle—*you cracked that fucker good with the hammer . . .*

In the quiet, Hudson can hear a slow buzzing thrum that he identifies as the faint sound of strings coming from Speck's headphones. Or maybe it's the pulsating blood in his head from getting so worked up. Hudson's brain does not assume that the noise is coming from the wasps that have been sneaking up from the bomb shelter running beneath the house ever since the hatch was busted wide. Hudson hears violin and viola and the faint sonorous wheeze of his brother's drunken sleep.

The young man stands tall. He makes his bed. Satisfied, he straightens his tie. By now, he hopes, the party is over. He doesn't feel badly about shirking his responsibilities. Although he's sorry that Gus is gone, he barely even knew him and can't really muster up any real sadness or grief. Hudson wonders, as he makes his way in the semi-light to the front door and exits, if this is how he's going to feel when his own old man passes.

Madison fights to shake off an echo of sadness that reverberates from the toppled chairs and damaged tent, the half-empty plastic wine cups and sodden crackers beside the glistening cheese. Down by the field the airplane's cockpit door stands open as an invitation.

The young woman was right there when Nolan slipped into his seizure. While the men pinned down his flailing appendages she steadied his head and neck to keep him from doing further damage to his tongue. The minister drove his car down and, with help, they loaded Nolan into the backseat. Clara rode in back as they sped to the hospital. Madison stayed behind for damage control. It was too late for her to do much more than apologize and thank folks for their sympathies. People were eager to leave.

Now, Madison stands in the twilight alone. Although she is exhausted she knows that she'll need to drive to the hospital for support. Off in the distance, tearing down the dirt path, she sees Pepper. The dog, against the dark, resembles a specter. It disappears into the hangar.

Back when the hangar was a barn and Madison was a young girl she used to climb inside the trucks and pretend she knew how to drive. There was one truck that nobody used that was eventually retired to the junkyard with the others, a harvester, and this was Madison's favorite hideout. She'd whittle away entire afternoons. Inside the cab with the warm scents of oil and gas and sweat, Madison felt safe. She kept her dolls in the glove box that she lined up in the passenger seat while she sat in the driver's seat and took them wherever they wanted to go—to the lake, the zoo, the drive-in, the pizza parlor, the moon. She could reach the pedals if she stretched, but then she wasn't able to see out the windshield. Most of the time she stayed perched on the seat and yanked the wheel from side to side making blubbering truck noises from her bunched lips. As she aged, she continued returning to the harvester. It was, at fourteen, a good place to smoke without getting caught. She would sit inside the cab with the windows rolled tight and practice inhaling. She kept her pink lighter and cigarettes in the glove box. Sometimes, out of boredom, she'd set her Barbie dolls on fire and let the intoxicating fumes cause her head to spin.

When her grandmother entered the barn that fall afternoon Madison didn't see her until she was several rungs up the ladder to the loft. There was nothing up there but empty crates and cobwebs so, slumping lower into the seat, Madison watched with curiosity. Dusk sunlight brought long shadows from the vine posts outside onto the hardened dirt of the barn floor. Madison tried to deduce why her grandmother would go up there. Even at fourteen the young girl was adept at figuring people out. She thought, *Maybe there's a secret treasure chest*, and, as the smoke seeped into the roof to add its scent with the others, the girl looked on with furtive excitement. It wasn't until Madison saw her grandmother's vacant and determined face and the coiled length of rope hitched over her shoulder that real fear set in. A bead of sweat trickled down her grandmother's nose, and she did not bother to swipe it away. Instead, she attempted to cast the rope over one of the exposed barn rafters. She missed on the first try. The rope snaked down and, hand-over-hand, the old woman retrieved it. She missed a second time. Four years have unspooled from that moment. After that second throw the girl *knew* what was happening. She could have said something. Screamed. Waved her arms. Burst from the truck.

Later, Madison visited a psychologist who emphasized a myriad of plausible reasons why an old woman with a brain tumor would choose to take her life. "The thing we need to remember," the psychologist stressed, "is that it's not your fault." Madison was instructed to write down, in her personal journal, *It's not my fault*, five hundred times every day for a month. Then she was allowed to reduce it to three hundred times every day for a month. Then two hundred. One. It didn't help. A thin bandage upon a slit wrist. Back then, Madison tells herself, if she knew that her granddaughter was huddled in the harvester below, wide-eyed and paralyzed, her grandmother would not have tried that third and successful time. The girl's eyes had followed the falling body on its interrupted way to the barn floor. Her grandmother didn't have time to pinch her own eyes shut or else didn't want to. For a while, and this is something she kept from the psychologist, Madison obsessed about the final image her grandmother saw before the twitching ceased. Her grandmother's head was eye-level with one of the open windows in the barn. Did she plan this? Could she see the red fields with the grapes ripe and ready? Or did her eyes roll downward? Did she spy Madison cowering in the truck with a nicotine-stained gaping mouth?

Afterward, in the silence, unable to move, Madison's ears were filled with the rhythmic creaking of the rope caught in the momentum of her grandmother's awkward leap. In the cab, unblinking eyes averted, she watched as the shadow from the body inched up the hood and to the dashboard. When it fell across the steering wheel the young girl pounded her clenched fists against the broken horn.

Madison shakes away a sudden chill. She rubs her hands vigorously up and down her arms. Then she's surprised to see someone walking towards her in the weak moonlight. She instinctively takes a step backward.

On his way to the main house to find out where everyone has gone Hudson notices Madison standing alone, in a trance. "Hey," he says, approaching. "You all right?"

"Yeah. I'm fine." Madison unfolds her arms. "I didn't know it was you. What are you still doing here?"

"I was with Speck. He's sick." Hudson does not feel like explaining what really happened and reveal how much of an incompetent older brother he has allowed himself to become.

"Oh. I can stay and watch him if you'd like to go to the hospital."

"What do you mean?"

"Your Dad. He collapsed. You didn't know?"

A wave of heat rises from his chest to his head. "No. What happened? Is he all right?"

"I really don't know," Madison says. "He chased a couple of kids into my grandfather's plane. I think they pissed him off."

"He was drunk," Hudson says.

"Maybe. I think he might have been trying to defend my mom. The Marauder means a lot to her. I'm going to drive over and be with them now."

Hudson squeezes his tongue in the space where his tooth used to be. He can see the precise place where Crowley beat him—ahead a few feet in the gravel. That moment seems so long ago.

"Your Dad visited my Mom when she was sick, after all. So did your brother."

Hudson's having a hard time concentrating. He's aware that Madison is implying something, but his brain just isn't sharp enough to figure it out. "I know. You're right. I'll get him. We'll meet you there. I can drive."

Madison frowns. She can't contain her disappointment. "Hey, what happened to that guy I met the other day? Where did you go? I liked him."

Hudson opens his mouth to explain. To find the right words. Madison doesn't wait. She turns her back and hurries to her car.

On his way to the pink house Hudson tries to muster the energy to care. To think—if only for himself—of the best way to articulate how he has become who he has become. He has always been adept at reasoning through relationships and behaving the way he believes others want him to. Speck once said that he reminded him of a chameleon. His little brother was right. While his appearances might mold to fit into the environment, beneath the skin his blood has been boiling.

When Hudson enters the house he first hears and then sees the wasps. They are crawling along the walls and ceiling. He has to blink a few times to make sure this is real. When the insects do not disappear, he rushes toward the bedroom in a panic.

At first, and it doesn't make sense, when Hudson sees the back of a figure looming over Speck in the bed he thinks of his father. "Dad?" he says. "Is that you?"

Then the man turns, and the off-centered cleft in his chin gives him away. Crowley's bloodshot, swollen eyes dart back and forth, processing the situation. He turns his thin lips into a wide grin. Two wasps sneak out the corners of his mouth and ping off the glass in the window before whirling around the room.

23.

Speck believes he is dreaming. Another night terror.

At first, his mother is running her hands soothingly through his hair and quelling a splitting headache. Beethoven's 9th isn't helping. When he opens his eyes he sees a monster crouching over him. There is blood staining the creature's face, and his crooked chin trembles with excitement. Speck pulls the covers tightly to his chest. When the monster opens his mouth the boy expects him to speak, to reprimand him for drinking the wine.

I know, I know, Speck mutters. *I'm sorry.*

The words that the boy knows he deserves—*You will pay for what you have done*—turn into tiny wasps as they trickle out of the monster's mouth and spiral away. The boy follows them, fascinated by how real they seem. The room spins and rotates.

Aren't they beautiful, little brother? the monster asks.

Yes, Speck says and then wonders why the monster has called him 'little brother.' This thing is not Hudson, is it? *No,* he says, *it can't be.*

The monster is taking off his shirt. His skin is made of brightly painted animals—a tiger, a wolf, a crow, a shark, a bear, a crocodile—and Speck reaches out to touch them. To make them come alive. But the monster isn't done. He removes his pants, too.

It can be, the monster insists.

The movement of the wasps slithering overhead on the ceiling makes Speck nauseous. *It's time to wake up,* he says. *You are not my brother.*

The monster lifts the covers and slides under them. *It doesn't matter who I am. It doesn't matter who you are. Half-brother plus half-brother equals a whole.*

It feels so real when the monster's rough fingers begin tugging away at his pajamas that the boy kicks and screams and shakes like he's electrified and tells himself, *Wake up, this is too much* as the monster's claws dig into his thighs, and the wasps dive bomb in a frenzy, and they begin stinging, *real* pain, under the control of the monster who is rising to his knees and preparing to devour the boy—*Wake up this is too much, wake up this is too much, wake up this is too much . . .*

"Dad?" Speck hears someone say. "Is that you?"

And Speck's not sure, though the monster isn't his father—his father is far, far away, out on the water where the dolphins chase the waves, and the seagulls sway with the gentle breeze, and the ship slices through the ocean spray, the mists of salt . . . but then, no, here, this is his brother, howling like a lunatic and attacking the monster. "Get him, get him, get him!" Speck shouts. And it works! The monster topples over. Hudson grabs the boy forcefully and holds him close, and now they're moving and so are the wasps. They dive down and sting, real pain, Speck feels— if this isn't a dream he doesn't know what it is—and they're outside, tripping down the porch, the boy's head is bobbing, *Yes, yes, yes,* looking backwards, and the wasps burst out of the house with the monster in hot pursuit—*We better hurry. Don't let him get us.*

I won't, Speck hears his brother say.

Is this real? the boy says because it feels that way.

Hudson doesn't answer. He's flying over the ground. The monster is having trouble keeping up. There's something wrong with the creature's legs, he's as slow as a zombie. All the jostling on his brother's shoulder, it's too much, and Speck gets sick down his brother's back—and there's no denying that he's awake, the burn of the wine on the throat coming back is not something that he can pretend away.

"I'm sorry," Speck manages through the stringy rivulets of spittle at his lips.

"Hold on," Hudson says. He pushes Speck onto the wing of the airplane and then scoots up himself. He drags his brother into the cockpit, throws himself inside, and slams the hatch shut, locks it. The wasps drum harmlessly against the glass windshield.

And Speck is thrilled by this turn of events, "I'm ready for takeoff!" he shouts.

Hudson isn't happy. He is sobbing into his hands, and the back of his head is quivering.

"Shh, shh," Speck says. "It's going to be all right." The boy wraps his arms around his brother and tries to rock him.

Outside, the monster screams and flails against the glass. Hudson's got his eyes pinched closed, but Speck keeps his open. Though he's frightened, he wants to confirm that this is real. And, sure enough, after a while, the monster turns into a man.

24.

That summer in Dwyer will go down as the hottest in history. As cooler years tick by and the peculiarities of those few weeks are not replicated people will blame the heat for that summer's curious circumstances. Warmer temperatures have been known to cause increased breeding in wasps which would explain the infestation in the Muller vineyard and surrounding area. With enough fumigation and the impending fall weather, the wasps disappeared and did not return.

Sweltering weather also causes people to act unusually. Makes people crazy. When authorities eventually found Crowley's body curled up in a ball beneath one of the airplane propellers they could clearly see that the man had been stung multiple times. Too much venom in the bloodstream triggers hallucinations. Plus, a whack in the head from a hammer can cause disorientation.

After Hudson came clean and admitted how he had been attacked by Crowley, which he needed to do in order to claim self-defense, he began to feel better. While it might be harder, it's healthier to drag the darkness into the light.

Police had to break down the door in the doublewide to get Ms. Crowley out and into assisted living. She'll tell nurses and authorities—anyone who will listen—what a monster her son James had been; she has countless examples. She has stories of Gabriel, too, what an angel he was and will always be in her memory and embodied in her menagerie.

Once sedated, doctors were able to operate on Nolan. While there was substantial damage to the inner ear, and he may experience compromised hearing for the rest of his life, Nolan was otherwise all right. The doctors weren't too surprised to pluck out the tiny, teeming wasp larvae and flush them down the drain. Bugs often crawl inside people's ears, get trapped, and sometimes they can cause serious, but not life threatening, damage.

Grapes grow back. The Muller vineyard will carry on. It will be a team effort. For five years Hudson and Madison will be stepbrother and sister. It will be awkward. They'll laugh nervously at the small wedding held on the vineyard, a ceremony much smaller than Gus's funeral party. Madison will be happy for her mother. She'll embrace Nolan as a stepfather without many reservations. She will, with a little coaxing, find out enough information about her biological father to track him down, make a call, and arrange for a meeting in Chicago where he lives with his family and is a successful chiropractor. Over time Madison will be part of her father's family.

Clara and Nolan won't need each other forever. When Nolan sheepishly admits he has an urge that he cannot repress—to move on—Clara will not put up much of a fight.

Returning home after that summer, Hudson will talk to his father every Sunday. At first, this will be a challenge since Nolan's tongue won't let him do much more than grunt into the receiver. Nolan will hold the phone to his good ear. Gradually they will find a rhythm. Hudson will get things off his chest and, uninterrupted, he will broach subjects he never could before—feelings of abandonment, pent up aggression due to unreasonable expectations, misunderstanding shrouding alcoholism—these emotions will spool out over the airways. Nolan will listen. Sometimes Hudson will believe that his father is sniffling and choking back tears on the other end. Even after the bandages come off and Nolan is capable of speaking, he will stay quiet, unwilling to stifle his son.

Speck will be encouraged by therapists to write down how he feels. At first, he won't know how to do this. He will be too full of resentment when nobody believes what really happened that summer. Nobody saw Tolly, and while there are twenty-one Leonard Tolly's who live in the New York City metropolitan area, none of them had any idea what Speck's parents—who were calling in order to appease their troubled boy—were talking about when presented with questions about wasps in Western New York. While there was a William Gent who lived in Rochester, the obituaries reported that he died in combat overseas and, when they pressed, Mr. and Mrs. Petro were told that the details surrounding the passing were classified. When this explanation did not satisfy Speck one of his child psychologists—the boy won't remember his name—will say, "There was no journal, Joshua."

"Yes, there was," he'll reply.

"All right," the doctor, undaunted, will say. "What was in it?"

Speck will recognize the doctor's placating tone and button up.

"Why don't you write it down? Write down what you remember."

Speck will be a good solider. He'll scribble away pointlessly for years and then, one morning, having grown into a man and with a child of his own, something will click. There is no reasonable explanation as to why he decides it is time to try and make sense of that summer nor is there reason to believe he is capable of doing so. The click that he hears in his head is the box opening and, like Pandora, he won't know what else to do but rummage around and hope for the best.

Joshua will take liberties with details. He'll stretch the truth paper thin. He'll not only have to imagine how he had been that hot summer— just a speck of a thing—he'll also have to imagine how his brother had been, how Mr. Baxter had been, and everything else. He'll spend a great deal of time shopping around for the closest replica of William Gent's black, leather-bound journal. Then he'll crack it open and in cursive write down what he remembers. *The solider pitches himself from the moving train. When he hits the ground his ankles turn, and he drops*, he'll begin. Then he'll keep going, all the way through.

All that, though, is years and years away. Now, on the porch of the faded red house, it is fall and today marks the anniversary of Elizabeth's passing.

Nolan manages to wrap his tongue and mouth around the words, "Are you ready?"

Clara has been daydreaming with her eyes on the new and barren horizon. The sun is setting slowly. Madison is roughhousing with Pepper in the dirt, waiting for them. In her lap Clara is holding an urn. She has combined her parents' ashes inside. The fields have been razed, dutifully. "Just about," she says absently, reaching into her shirt pocket and fishing out a cigarette.

Without missing a beat Nolan pulls out his lighter and lifts it to her lips. "They'll grow back stronger," he struggles to say. "Your parents will see to it." Nolan rolls his thumb across the lighter-wheel, but cannot get it lit. He tries again, and again, leaning close enough to embrace her.

"Don't worry about it," Clara says.

"No. Wait here."

Nolan enters the house. With the windows open the lingering scent from the insecticide fumes is all but gone. When they finished inspecting the house the officials left it nice and neat. The place looks cleaner than it ever has.

On the mantle are the boxes. In the smallest, cherry-colored coffin-shaped box with engraved flowers and a pewter top are the matches. From time to time in the winter he'll build a fire. Nolan reaches in and plucks a stick out. Even if he peered in and closely scrutinized the contents of the box the man would have trouble differentiating the withered tick carcasses from the red tips of the matchsticks. He would have no way of knowing that the queen wasp Speck left in the confined dark safety of the box laid her eggs. When hatched, the hungry wasp larvae evolved. The tiny parasites fought one another and drained every last drop of blood from the engorged ticks. Only the strongest few survived. Together, they pushed at the lid, yearning to stretch their wings. Then, they turned on each other. Exhausted and famished the sole survivor burrowed beneath the pile of matches to wait for the light or else death. Nolan can't see the frantic struggle the adolescent wasp is making, so desperate to be free.

Before it can escape Nolan replaces the heavy pewter top.

Casting his eyes to the window the man notices that it is much darker outside than it was when he entered. He's not sure how this happened, how he overlooked such a dramatic change in light. The wind billows in the sheer curtains. A sudden crush of sadness collapses upon him. He's not sure what to make of it. Maybe some remnant from the old man above. The only way he knows how to combat the way he feels is to focus on the task laid out before him. He runs the match along the coarse mantle wood until the head catches and pops alive. Cupping his shaky hand, Nolan carries the delicate flame out onto the porch.

Acknowledgments

Thanks to Jon Fink for his steadfast belief, patience, and encouragement.

Thanks to my grandfather, Frank Ockert, for finding his way home from the war.

And thanks to Dawn, Gavin, and Jayden for everything good in this world. Without you, I'm not.

JASON OCKERT is the author of two collections of short stories: *Neighbors of Nothing* and *Rabbit Punches*. He has received awards from the *Atlantic Monthly*, Mary Roberts Rinehart Foundation, and the Dzanc Short Story collection contest, and he has been nominated for a Shirley Jackson Award. His short fiction has appeared in *New Stories from the South, Best American Mystery Stories, Oxford American, storySouth, Ecotone, The Iowa Review, One Story, McSweeney's,* and *Post Road*. He teaches at Coastal Carolina University.

CPSIA information can be obtained at www.ICGtesting.com
Printed in the USA
BVOW08s1136080315

390783BV00004B/51/P